LONESOME VAGABOND

Ann El-Nemr

LONESOME VAGABOND
ANN EL-NEMR

Published September 2015
Little Creek Books
Imprint of Jan-Carol Publishing, Inc.
All rights reserved

ISBN: 978-1-939289-72-8
Library of Congress Control Number: 2015952269

You may contact the publisher:
Jan-Carol Publishing, Inc.
PO Box 701
Johnson City, TN 37605
E-mail: publisher@jancarolpublishing.com
Website: jancarolpublishing.com

Jan-Carol
Publishing, Inc
"every story needs a book"

To all the people who love to sit back
and enjoy a great book on a lazy afternoon.

LETTER TO THE READER

Well, here we are again. This book *Lonesome Vagabond* was a lot of fun to write since I started to conceive this project while I was visiting several islands in the Caribbean last winter. My mind never stops thinking about telling my readers a new intriguing story. My novels are, as always, a love story first; but as you might already know there is a component of suspense in every tale I write. This time around it's centered around two brothers, Riker and Logan who are complete opposites.

Riker is a power hungry CEO who wants to run their empire and his sibling's life. Logan is fed up with his brother's dominant behavior and sets out for a simple life, traveling the Caribbean islands aboard his yacht, in search of love. He encounters Bailey on the beach in Barbados. Logan is determined to seduce her without telling her how rich he really is, but things don't always work like one wants and when Riker comes to visit Logan on his boat, he immediately despises Bailey. He believes she is out to get his brother's fortune and will do anything in his power to break them up. I never know the ending of my novels until the last chapters. I will tell you this. The story has a tragic end for one of the characters. Which one? You will have to read the novel to the end! Enjoy!

ACKNOWLEDGMENTS

I would like to thank all the people who have supported my new career; especially my fans. There is nothing more fulfilling than hearing the enthusiasm in readers' voices when they tell me how much they enjoy reading my novels. I truly value every word.

INTRODUCTION

I just want to say a few words to my readers about how much your feedback is appreciated. Your positive comments push me to become better at my craft. I love to entertain your minds, to make you forget for a short time your surroundings, and let you become part of my stories. A good novel can distract you from all the worries of daily life. This is what I strive to do with every book I write.

CHAPTER 1

Bailey wiggled her toes as she moved her feet back and forth in the hot sand. She lay on her back with her knees bent; she felt the sun beating down on her skin. She could hear the sound of the waves resonating in her ears. Her mind was occupied with her recent shattered relationship.

Bailey worked as a secretary for a veterinary clinic, and had used her savings to take a few weeks off from work to try to put her life together again. She needed to be away from Martin, and try to forget him.

She was on a small private beach in Barbados, where she should've been taking advantage of this vacation and having a good time. Her best friend, Dakota, booked this cruise for a change of scenery. She hoped to encounter a new love interest.

But, she couldn't stop thinking how alone she felt since the break-up with her long-time boyfriend, Martin. He was her first and only true love. They met at the animal clinic where she worked when he brought his dog in for shots. He asked her out to dinner that same day. She remembered how excited she had been. She didn't have a man in her life at the time, and liked Martin the minute she met him. So when he asked her out, she accepted immediately. They started dating regularly.

Now at thirty-two, she didn't think she would ever find love again. The thought of having a family had been ruined. She felt so depressed that it was difficult to concentrate on work or her social life. She had cried until there were no more tears. What had gone wrong? Why? She had given him everything, wasting seven years of her life. She blamed herself, though. Maybe she could have saved the relationship if she had been more attentive to his needs, or hadn't worked such long hours. "Stop it!" She told herself as tears swam in her eyes behind her sunglasses.

A tear slowly slipped from her eye down her right cheek. She reached up with her hand and discreetly wiped it away with her index finger. She blinked several times, pushing them away. She opened her eyes and rose upon her elbows when she noticed a beautiful yacht anchored near by in the water. How lucky can some people be?

She shook her head as she watched her best friend, Dakota cool off from the heat in the water of the Caribbean Sea. Their small, luxurious ship held only two hundred people on board. She had agreed to come along as long as it was only for fun, not to go meet another man, she remembered.

"I'll go under one condition. You are not to fix me up with men. I really don't need that right now. It's a girls' trip, okay?" Bailey told her suspiciously, as she laughed. Dakota crossed her arms in front of her and grinned at her friend.

"You're no fun, but if that's the only way I can get you to go, let's book it," she answered, laughing.

This cruise was scheduled to travel to seven different islands in the Caribbean Sea in a two-week span. It seemed like a good idea at the time, but now Bailey was kind of sorry because she had too much time to think.

Bailey saw Dakota waving her hands. She was signaling Bailey to come into the water. She looked around her surroundings, trying to ignore Dakota as she noticed the people to her right playing volleyball on the sand while others were eating or sunbathing.

"Come on, Bailey it's beautiful," Dakota yelled at her from the water. She kept dunking in and out like a fish. Bailey nodded, then rose from her towel and walked to the edge of the surf. She took a few steps into the water, then stopped.

"It's not that cold, you chicken shit," Dakota shouted. She was laughing at Bailey, with her hands on her hips. "I'm coming," Bailey answered. She continued walking a little further into the water as her feet sank into the sand. The coldness of the waves on her skin gave her goosebumps. She finally found the courage to dip under the water but quickly stood up, shivering. She'd cried out when the water engulfed her body. Bailey rubbed her arms with her hands. Dakota, dripping wet, walked over and stood next to her.

"Now, don't you think it feels better, and how the hell do you think you are going to meet a man by just laying in the sun, girl? You need to be seen, get it?" she told her. Dakota stuck her tongue out at Bailey playfully. They both giggled. Bailey shook her head, then splashed cold water on her friend.

"Okay, okay," Bailey said. "Fine, let's go to the bar and get a drink," she said, as she retreated from the water. They slipped on their cover-ups, gathered their beach towels and sunscreen, and slowly strolled to the bar hut. Bailey and Dakota pulled a seat out from the bamboo counter and sat down in the shade. It was an outdoor bar with a straw roof, one counter, and a dozen wicker seats. The staff of the cruise ship had set it up for refreshments for the patrons of the ship.

"Could we have two piña coladas, please?" Dakota asked, before she put her bag on the bar counter.

"Look to your left," Dakota whispered in her ear. She turned her head, but only noticed a gentleman in his fifties drinking a beer. Dakota elbowed Bailey lightly.

"Why did you elbow me, you goof?" Bailey asked, taking her drink from the bartender.

"You are horrible! Look over there, at the other end of the bar," she murmured, then tilted her head toward the man. "What man?" Bailey asked her. She scanned the area again. She spotted him this time. Handsome, she thought, as she peeked at him. His purple t-shirt hugged his biceps to perfection and there wasn't much room left in his fitted, cut-off denim shorts. He had shoulder-length curly blond hair that moved with the breeze. His golden skin seemed to glisten in the sun. He reminded her of a real beach bum. His eyes were directly on her. Suddenly he slowly tipped his head and smiled at her. She quickly turned her head away, embarrassed, having been caught staring at him. She bowed her head and looked at her drink.

"You are oblivious to everything, aren't you? He's been watching you since you walked to the bar," Dakota informed her.

"Now, I'm going to the ladies room. I'll be back. Smile, will you?" Dakota told her. Bailey reached out to grab her arm to stop Dakota from leaving her alone, but she missed and Dakota walked away. She knew what she was doing. She left Bailey by herself so she might meet this man. Bailey started playing with her napkin, folding the corners. She casually cast her eyes toward the man again. His eyes were still on her, and he grinned her way. Surprised, her mouth opened. She turned her head to avoid his stare, wondering where the hell Dakota was. She shifted her weight in her seat while scanning the opposite area for her friend.

"Hi. Do you mind if I join you?" she heard a smooth male voice beside her. She whipped her head around to see who it was. Her hand accidently hit her glass, spilling her drink on the counter. She immediately jumped back to stand up, reaching over to grab a bunch of napkins to stop the drink from spilling on her chair. Taking no notice of the man who had spoken to her while grabbing for napkins, she realized someone was still beside her a few seconds later. He tried to help her by also grabbing napkins and soaking up the mess. His hand bumped into hers while wiping the counter. She froze as she looked up at him.

"I'm so sorry. Did it get on you?" she managed to ask. Her wet napkins were still dripping in her hand. Not a muscle moved as she gawked at him. Wow! He had deep blue eyes, which seemed as though they were reading her mind, and long, blonde eye lashes. She couldn't tear her eyes away. She was brought out of her trance when he touched her arm. She cast her eyes to the side. A chill ran down her back. "Sorry!" was all she could mumble. She felt the heat rise to her face as she sat her butt down on the edge of the stool and looked at her empty glass.

"Two more drinks, please," she heard his husky voice say to the bartender.

Try to get a grip and not make a fool of yourself again, Bailey, she thought, feeling embarrassed.

"I'll start again, may I join you?" she heard him ask again. She glanced up. He was pointing at the seat beside her. She sneaked another look his way.

"Sure, but only if you let me pay for the drinks," she managed to say. She watched the bartender approach and place two ice cold drinks in front of them. He gently pushed one of them toward her hand, smiled at her, and seized the other drink.

"Thank you." It was all she could say since she was paralyzed by his panache. He lifted his drink up and said, "Chin, chin." She picked up her drink and gently tapped his glass. He took a sip, pulled out the bar-stool, and sat down. He rotated his body toward her. His knees bumped her leg, but she noticed he didn't move them away—neither did she. It felt nice to be so close to a man again.

"My name is Logan St. James," he said, with another smile showing his perfect white teeth. He extended his hand to her.

"Oh! My name is Bailey, Bailey Winters," she said, and lifted her hand to his. He had a nice grip. He held her hand for an extra moment. She softly pulled her hand away.

"So, how do you like the cruise?" she asked. A crewmember had told her that this particular beach was reserved for the ship members, but she had not seen him onboard.

"Ahhh, I'm not on the cruise. I just came by to get refreshments," he answered. He changed the subject. She didn't question it; she figured he probably lived on the island.

"Is this your first time in Barbados?" he asked as he examined her.

"Yes," was all she could say. My God! Bailey, get your act together.

"Are you having a good time?" he asked. His attention was totally focused on her.

"It's okay. It was my girlfriend's idea that I tag along, so yes, it's fun to be able to spend time with her. We're planning to go out to dinner tonight at this small restaurant called The Tides. Do you know it?" she asked him. She took a gulp from her drink. She felt the cold liquid go down to her stomach.

"Yes, I do know it. I've dined there many times. Excellent food. You should make sure to be seated outside, by the boardwalk. It's kind of interesting to watch the people go by," he answered. He hadn't taken his eyes off her for a second.

"I'll have to ask the maître d' to seat us there," she said. Where was Dakota? She'd been gone what seemed like an eternity. Bailey searched the area with her eyes, looking for her. Finally she saw Dakota coming out of the ladies room.

"Great! So tell me, what islands you are going to visit?" he questioned. He seemed distracted, looking past her shoulder.

"Well, this is our last night in Bridgetown. We're sailing to St. Lucia tonight, St. George tomorrow, and..." She tapped her finger on her chin, trying to remember the others.

"I'm not sure about the others. I just take one port at a time. My friend would know. She's very good at organizing our trip. I'm just not sure," she answered, then felt someone's hand on her back.

6

"Hey! Where's my drink?" she heard Dakota say as she sat down beside her. Surprised, Bailey turned toward her. Dakota had crept up beside her unseen.

"Hi, I'm Dakota," she said as she waved her hand to get the bartender's attention. She motioned for another drink when he saw her. She made herself comfortable and crossed her legs.

"This is Logan St. James," Bailey introduced him. They both nodded at each other.

"I just talked to one of the stewards. He told me the shuttle to re-board the ship was leaving in about twenty minutes," Dakota told Bailey.

"Okay, it will give us time to relax before we return to the island for dinner," Bailey answered. She was a bit disappointed that she didn't have more time to get to know this man.

"Bailey just told me you were going to The Tides tonight for dinner. It's a charming restaurant. What time are your reservations?" Logan inquired as he finished the last of his drink.

"We're suppose to be there around eight o'clock, I think. Right?" Bailey answered. She glanced with a nod at Dakota for confirmation. Logan smiled at both of them.

"I hope you enjoy your dinner. They make great food. It was nice to meet you, Bailey. Thanks for the drink. Next time it's on me, Dakota," he said, patting Bailey's hand. He stood up and was about to leave when Dakota asked, "Why don't you join us?"

"Dakota! I'm sure he has better things to do than team up with us," Bailey exclaimed as she lightly elbowed her friend, startled at her outburst. Dakota just made a face at her and looked at Logan.

"I'd love to," Logan answered quickly. Bailey's mouth fell open in surprise, but she closed it immediately. She was delighted she would see him again.

"Great! We'll be there around eight. Come on Bailey, we have a shuttle to catch," Dakota said. She put her beach bag strap over her shoulder and stood up. Bailey smiled at Logan, and he returned it.

"See you later," she told Logan, waving goodbye. She walked away toward the small dock, where a small boat was waiting to take them back to their ship. She felt as if she was being watched, so she turned to look back at the bar hut for one last peek at Logan, but he was nowhere to be seen.

***

Logan was excited by the prospect of seeing Bailey again. His heartbeat had accelerated when he first spotted her lying on her towel on the beach, but he'd hesitated to approach her until he saw her going toward the bar. She was more beautiful close up, with those hazel eyes and long black hair. It had been his best chance. He thought he saw her wipe a tear away while watching her earlier, but he wasn't sure. He loved how she blushed when she spilled the drink, making her even more desirable. She wasn't like the girls he usually encountered. She seemed a bit insecure, reminding him of a child's innocence. The women he usually met were very aggressive when getting to know him, not because of who he was, but because of his fortune. He had never asked for it, but his grandmother had left him and his twin brother her wealth after her death. She'd been the hotel queen of New York, with an estimated worth of over eight hundred million dollars in real estate alone.

His mind reverted back to when Bailey sat at the bar. She looked shy, unsure of herself, and humble. She wasn't decked out in designer clothes, and she didn't seem to be looking to capture a man's heart. Her long black hair was tied up into a ponytail, and those full lips were mouthwatering. He had an urge to just lean forward while she sat next to him and kiss her mouth. He couldn't wait to see her again. His gut feeling told him she was special. He watched her walk away, her hips swaying from side to side, until she disappeared around the building.

He boarded his yacht anxious about seeing her again. He had butterflies in his stomach. She was the first person in a long time whom he was really curious about. He needed to know more about her. He absolutely wanted to know everything about her. He had to make a good impression tonight. He wasn't going to tip his hand and tell her who he really was until he was sure she was the one. He didn't believe in love at first sight, but...

He was thirty-one years old, single, and basically lived a vagabond lifestyle, going from one place to another. Drifting island to island without a fixed agenda had become his life. His brother Riker had called him a playboy. What did he know? They were complete opposites.

Logan never wanted to be a CEO of this empire, so he was content letting his brother Riker run the company. As a matter of fact, Riker wanted to rule everything—even Logan's love life. He was always telling Logan whom he should date or hang out with. That's why he had left New York. He hated those opulent, hungry types of people, always pushing themselves on him for one reason: his money. Riker wanted him to take a more active role in the company so he could dictate Logan's life. Not being part of the business gave Logan time to do what he loved to do, go sailing and fishing. But lately he'd become aware of an emptiness inside, feeling more alone. Maybe he should return to work, but all he could hear was his brother's voice screaming at him: "What the hell did you do that for?" "You couldn't be that stupid!" "Take her out, she's perfect for you." Those thoughts and more had kept him away. His brother was a ruthless, domineering man. He didn't show any remorse when firing someone or bullying his way into what he desired.

CHAPTER 2

Bailey stood in front of the mirror in her cramped suite. It consisted of a single bed, a tiny desk with a chair, a bathroom that you could barely turn around in, and barely enough room to walk between them. How lucky was she, to have a porthole to look outside? It didn't even open, but thank God she really didn't spend too much time here, except to sleep and change her clothes.

She smoothed the front of her pink, white-flowered, strapless dress with her hand. It had a few wrinkles from being tucked in the suitcase. She had taken a nap, so now didn't have time to iron it. Dakota would be at her door in less than five minutes. She had the jitters, thinking of seeing Logan again. Who was she kidding? He probably had a girl in every port, ha! He wasn't the type of man she usually dated, but then she hadn't been dating at all lately.

Martin had swept her off her feet. She'd never thought after seven years together she would ever be single again. She couldn't save their relationship, even though she would always love him. Maybe Martin didn't want the relationship saved. He betrayed her trust for another woman. No, not betrayed, killed her faith in men. She eventually found out he had been having an affair for the last three years of their romance. "No darling, I can't make it tonight, I'm working late."

"Sorry, I'm late. I forgot about dinner." "I'll make it up to you. I have to go on this business trip."

Tears welled up as she remembered all the excuses he gave her over the years. What a fool she had been! All those years thrown away, and for what? She touched her chest with her palm as if she was being stabbed in the heart every time she revisited it. She shook her head, blinked her tears away, reached over and grabbed her clutch. She decided to meet her friend instead of drowning in her sorrow; it was time to move on. She was a strong, confident woman so she held her head up, opened the door, and with long strides headed toward Dakota's room.

She stood in front of her friend's door and knocked lightly. She waited, but the door didn't open.

"Dakota, it's me. Open the door," she said impatiently as she shifted her weight from one foot to the other. She heard moaning sounds coming from the cabin. She looked down the hall then placed her ear to the door. "Dakota, are you all right?" she asked, now concerned. She cupped the doorknob and turned it, but it was locked. "Dakota?" she said louder. She pounded on the door with her fist. "Coming," she finally heard Dakota say. The door swung open. She watched as Dakota shuffled back to her bunk and flopped down on it.

"My God Dakota! Are you okay, you look horrible, what's the matter?" Bailey asked. She approached her friend and sat at the edge of her bed. She noticed Dakota was pale and her skin was clammy. Bailey laid her palm on her forehead, "No fever, at least. That's good."

"I'm not sure, but I must have eaten something that wasn't good. My stomach is upset and I'm so nauseous," she said, rubbing her belly.

"Did you throw up?" Bailey asked. She got up, went to the mini bar, and poured some ginger ale in a paper cup.

"Here, sip some of this." Bailey handed Dakota the soda. She took a small drink and gave Bailey the cup back.

"I just need to rest, I'll be just fine," she said, closing her eyes.

"Try to sleep; you'll feel better when you wake up. I'll go change and be right back," Bailey told her as she stood up.

"No, no, you go to the restaurant without me," Dakota said, turning on her side.

"Are you crazy? I'm not leaving you to go meet a strange man I just met. You're sick," Bailey answered.

"NO! I want you to go. I just need to sleep. What are you going to do, sit and watch me sleep? Now go! I'll be fine," she told her, not moving.

"I really don't want to go anymore, not without you, plus you don't feel well," Bailey said in a low tone. She squeezed Dakota's upper arm.

"Do me a favor and go. I'll be fine. I'll text you if I get worse, how's that? Logan will be there to keep you company. I saw the way he looked at you this afternoon," she said. Bailey bit her lower lip, debating what she should do. Dakota opened her eyes and looked up at her, then gave her a weak smile.

"You look pretty, now please go and have fun."

"Fine, it's no use arguing with you. I'll go. I won't be late. I'll come check on you as soon as I get back," Bailey told her as she opened the door to walk away. She saw Dakota nodding at her and giving her a thumbs up.

Bailey felt guilty leaving her alone, but she knew Dakota would never stop bugging her to go to dinner. Maybe all she needed was to get a bit of shut-eye to bounce back. She'd peek in on Dakota when she returned from the restaurant.

She strolled down to the pier and flagged a taxi. She sat in the back seat wondering if she would be dining alone, or if Logan would really show up. Either way, she told herself, she would have a nice meal. The cab pulled up in front of The Tides restaurant. Bailey paid the driver, got out of the taxi, and had stepped toward the front door when she heard her name called. Surprised, she turned. To her delight, Logan was standing beside her. Her heart started to beat faster and she instantly smiled when she saw him. *"Wow,"* she thought to herself. He looked amazing, in a white linen shirt and black pants. His hair was slicked back with gel, and she could smell a musky fragrance emitting from him.

"Hi. You look beautiful. So where's your friend, Dakota?" he asked her, brushing his hand on her arm. His touch sent a shiver down her spine. She just stared at him for a second, not uttering a word. "Oh! Hi, I'm sorry, thank you, I...umm...she couldn't make it. She wasn't feeling well, but wanted me to come anyway," she answered him. Her eyes darted toward the front door as she held her clutch tighter, not moving.

"That's too bad. I hope she feels better soon. Shall we?" he asked as he extended his arm. Bailey smiled at him again, but did not slip her arm into his. Instead she casually walked to the entrance and he followed. A doorman opened the carved wooden doors for them.

"Welcome to The Tides," Bailey heard him say. She approached the reception area and stopped. "Good evening, do you have reservation?" the blonde lady asked them pleasantly.

"Yes, the name is Dakota Baker," Bailey answered. She could feel the heat of Logan's body next to hers. The young woman, wearing a black dress, looked at the appointment book before grabbing two menus.

"Follow me please," she said, and led them into the dining area. She placed the menus on the table and said, "Enjoy your dinner," and walked away.

"This is a nice place," Bailey said, as she took her seat facing the beach. She watched Logan as he sat beside her. His knees briefly touched hers as he pulled his chair forward. A bit taken back by the contact of his leg, she quickly jerked her leg away. She quickly turned her face away to examine the area, hoping he hadn't detected it.

The restaurant had an area open to the outside with mahogany chairs and snowy white tablecloths on the tables. What intrigued Bailey were the trees. There were four large tree trunks standing in the dining area that went through the roof of the restaurant.

Crystal glasses and platinum silverware were placed expertly on the table, complimented by a black cloth napkin. Soft classical music played in the background. She noticed people walking hand in hand down the boardwalk lining the outside perimeter of the restaurant by the beach. Bailey could smell the sea breeze as the wind gently blew on her.

She was brought back to reality when she felt a hand on hers. She bent her head down and slowly pulled it away to grab her menu. She was nervous being alone with a man she didn't know.

"Isn't it beautiful?" he asked. His eyes were locked on her. She opened her menu, pretending to scan it, but she was just staring at the letters.

"Yes, it is," she answered, not moving her eyes away from the page. *"Stop being so rigid and cold for God sake!"* she told herself.

"I recommend the catch of the day. It's usually mahi-mahi or barracuda. That is, if you like fish?" he said. She looked up at him. His hand was on top of her menu, pulling it down so he could see her face. He smiled at her. She closed her menu and placed it in front of her on the table.

"That sounds perfect," she answered with a weak smile.

"Red wine all right? Unless you prefer something else," he said, without moving. His eyes were still locked on her. Bailey just nodded. She could feel her heart pounding. *"Relax!"* she told herself, *"he doesn't bite!"*

"Wine would be great," she managed to say. Her mouth was parched as she crossed her fingers tightly on her knees. The waiter greeted them and took their order. They both decided to try the fish. She watched as he requested a bottle of Opus One 2011. The waiter nodded at him, and then smiled as if he'd known that would be what Logan would order. Strange!

"Very well, sir," he answered Logan. She was making too much of it; the waiter turned and walked away. They were alone once again.

"So, we didn't have much time to talk this afternoon. Tell me about yourself. How are you enjoying your cruise?" he casually asked her. He tilted his head, placed his elbow on the edge of the table, and rested his chin on his hand.

"There isn't much to say. I'm single, and I work in a veterinary clinic in a small town outside Boston. I would like to open an animal shelter one day, but until then..." she stopped talking and shrugged her shoulders. She cast her sight to the patrons who were being seating next to her. She was brought back to the conversation when she heard him clear his throat. She turned her attention back to him, embarrassed, and continued.

"I took a few weeks off; Dakota encourage me to take time off to tag along on this cruise. What about you?" She'd rather talk about him, so she gave the ball back to him.

"Well, I'm happy you tagged along, otherwise we wouldn't have met. I'm from New York, but I presently live on a boat I bought a few years back. I decided to roam around the islands for a few months," he said as the waiter arrived with their wine. *Thank God! I really need something to drink.* She watched as Logan tasted the wine. After the server poured wine in each glass, she slowly reached over for hers as he said, "To a wonderful evening, Bailey. I'm glad you decided to tag along, otherwise I wouldn't have met you." He raised his glass. Bailey nodded and took a sip. She could feel the sand lifting away from her tongue with the smooth taste of the wine, which had a hint of cherry. She couldn't help herself. She raised her glass once again to take another mouthful.

"Good wine!" she said. "So tell me, what kind of work do you do?" she asked, wondering how he could take off that much time.

"I'm in real estate. What do you do at the veterinary clinic?" he asked, then sipped his wine.

"I love animals, so I became a veterinary secretary. It's great! The animals make me laugh all the time." A sad thought passed through her mind as she pondered if she would ever have her own animal shelter. She took another sip of her wine, which seemed to be calming her soul.

"What islands will you be traveling next on this cruise?" he asked again as the waiter headed to the table with their meals. Before she answered, the waiter placed their entrées on the table.

"I'm not sure. Dakota has the schedule, but I think we are here for another day, then St. Lucia and St. George. After that, I'm not sure. Why?" She grabbed her fork and took a bite of her mahi-mahi. Her eyes were focused on her plate. She lifted her gaze for a second to look at him. Logan had not touched his food. He was observing her every move. Bailey could feel heat rising to her face. Her mouth opened a bit, then she closed it. He was still looking directly at her. She watched as the corners of his mouth turned up into a grin. She took another gulp of wine. She felt it go all the way to her stomach. The alcohol wasn't helping. She knew she was blushing. Bailey looked away, then she repositioned her feet under her chair. She giggled nervously as she grasped her fork once more.

"Could you stop staring at me and eat?" she whispered. She bent her head down, but she could feel his gaze still on her.

"You are stunning! And I love the way you laugh and blush," he told her as he picked up his utensil.

"The food is delicious. Eat, before it gets cold," was all she could say. She heard him chuckle quietly. The rest of the evening went well. She talked about her travels and her work; he told her about his sailing and how he loved to fish, among other things. Two hours later, they were still talking. She found that she loved the way he tilted his head and folded his hands on the table when he listened to her. He snatched the check as soon as the server put it on the table, even though she strongly objected.

"You can buy the next time," he joked. He reached into his pocket and threw his credit card into the folder. He waved the waiter down and the waiter took it immediately.

As if that was going to happen. I'll probably never see him again! She was on a cruise from one country to another. He was sailing around the Caribbean.

He asked the server to telephone a taxi for her. They strolled out of the dining area, then stood and waited in the front of the restaurant for the cab to arrive. She could feel him next to her, and his musky aroma invaded her nostrils. She felt his hand around her waist, paralyzing her. She couldn't move or speak. She just looked straight ahead. She could feel his fingers fanning her back. The taxi drove up and stopped. "Shall we?" She heard him say. Puzzled, she turned to face him. His hand dropped down from her waist to her side.

"You don't have to accompany me to the ship, I'll be fine. Thank you for the dinner," she said, as calmly as she could. She started to extend her hand to shake his, but he gently pulled her against his body. His arms wrapped around her body. She couldn't move, she was too shocked. Her mouth was inches from his; she looked into his eyes. She was very aware of his hard body against hers. He lowered his lips to her mouth and kissed her, ever so softly. A shiver passed down her back at the moment his lips touched hers. She wanted more, but still didn't dare move.

"You are welcome," he said, then released her. She just stood there startled. He had kissed her. He grabbed the handle and opened the back door of the cab. "Thank you," she said and slipped into the seat, still feeling stunned by what had just happened. She hadn't expected it, but she was delighted. She looked at him standing by the door. Suddenly he motioned to her to roll down her window.

She pressed the button and the window slid down. Logan bent down near the opening. "I'll see you soon," he said and took a step back. The only thing she could do was nod, as the taxi took off towards the pier. He disappeared out of view.

CHAPTER 3

Logan stood on the curb of the entrance of the restaurant watching the taxi drive away until he couldn't see it anymore. He felt an empty feeling rush over him. He placed his hands in his pockets and closed his eyes to keep her image fresh in his mind. He thought about how he liked it when she blushed. Her soft voice made him want to kiss her all over.

He needed to see her again. She brought life into him. He strolled down the street where he had parked his Harley motorcycle. Why hadn't he offered to drive her back to the ship? *I could have had more time with her! I could be feeling her warm body pressing against mine.* He reached over and unlocked his helmet from the seat and placed it on his head. He lifted up the plastic visor and buckled the strap under his chin before swinging his right leg over the body of the bike and sitting down on the seat. He took his key out of his pocket and placed it into the slot to start the motor. He pushed the stand up with his foot. Logan definitely wanted to see more of Bailey. He took off toward Bridgetown, where his deckhand awaited his return, to board his yacht.

A half hour later he was back aboard *The Vagabond*, his home. He walked up to the top deck of the ship to the bar area and poured himself a whiskey in a tumbler. He grasped the glass tightly in his hand and within a few steps he was on the stern of the boat. He sat down on one of the cushioned deck chairs overlooking the Bridgetown pier. He could see Bailey's ship, all lit up with white lights. He wondered if she was thinking of him. He tapped his fingers against the arm of the chair. "She has one more day in Barbados, tomorrow," she had said. He raised his tumbler to his lips and took a big sip of his drink. He felt it burn all the way down. His eyes felt heavy as they started to close. He would find her in the morning. How difficult could it be? The island wasn't that big.

He rose from his spot and walked to the intercom, then pushed the button to summon his private steward, Henry. Henry was his butler, a master in martial arts, his personal bodyguard when he was needed, and his confidant. He could always find the information he needed to protect Logan from his brother. But most of all, Henry was a longtime friend. He waited by the bar, pouring himself another drink. He lifted his head and saw Henry approaching him. He was dressed in his usual attire, white shirt and blue pants.

Henry was an older gentleman, in his early fifties, and had never married. He was the only person who truly knew Logan. He had been with him since his early teens; first as his private butler, later as his companion and personal bodyguard. His grandmother had appointed Henry because she was always very protective of her grandchildren after the death of their parents. Logan chose him as his chief steward of his yacht. Henry always believed him when he tried to defend himself from his brother's actions, especially when Riker blamed him for everything from lying to stealing. Henry was his only true friend. He was a very resourceful man who knew a lot of people. Henry had been traveling with Logan for the last ten years around the world, and since he had bought *The Vagabond.*

"Good evening, sir. How may I help you?" Henry asked politely as he stood in front of Logan with his hands clasped behind him.

"Henry, I need you to do me a favor tomorrow morning. I met this young lady today on the island. She is onboard the Windstar ship at the pier. Her name is Bailey Winters. Could you have two dozen red roses delivered to her cabin?" Logan asked, as he looked in the direction of the ship.

"No, problem sir, what would you like the card to say?" Henry asked him as he picked up a piece of paper and pen.

"Um, thank you for a wonderful...no, lovely, evening," he said, unsure as he stared toward her ship once again.

"Anything else, sir?" Henry asked as he waited by the counter. Logan brought his hand toward his face and tapped his index finger upon his chin. He glanced quickly at Henry then asked, "Could you discreetly find out where she will be tomorrow, I mean, what excursion she might have booked? I'd like to see her again." A small smile appeared on Henry's face.

"No problem, sir. I'm sure that I can find out," he answered.

"Thanks, Henry. Let me know as soon as you find out," Logan said. Henry nodded, turned and walked toward the bow of the boat to carry out his duties. Logan raised his tumbler and took one last sip. He placed his glass on the bar and headed downstairs to his stateroom, wondering if Henry could acquire the information he had asked for. Henry had never disappointed him. *Why didn't I ask her where she would be for dinner tomorrow night? How stupid of me!* He had been so caught up with her, the question had eluded him.

He shed his clothes, lay on top of his bed, stretched his arms behind his head, and closed his eyes, remembering Bailey's smile. He couldn't wait for sleep to invade his thoughts so that it would be tomorrow.

***

Bailey went straight to her friend's room when she got back on the ship. She took long strides until she stood in front of Dakota's door.

She was breathing hard from almost running down to the lower deck, her heart beating harder than usual as she raised her hand and knocked on the door.

"Dakota, it's me, open the door," Bailey uttered in great haste. The door swung open, Dakota motioning her in.

"So, tell me how was dinner?" she inquired then turned around to sit on a chair.

"It was good, he was polite, funny, just like a gentleman," she told her as she sat on the edge of Dakota's bed. Even though she wanted to scream all the details at her friend, she held her tongue.

"How are you feeling?" Bailey asked. Bailey saw Dakota's eyes dance. She suddenly knew Dakota had been faking. Dakota turned her face away.

"You little faker, you're not sick at all, are you?" Bailey slapped her arm. Dakota pulled away, laughing.

"Okay, I just wanted you to go out on a date. I saw how you looked at him," she said, "Dish! How was it? I want details." They looked at each other and started to giggle, just like they used to do in their younger days.

"Well, we met at the front entrance, he looked delicious, and we were seated..." she was interrupted by Dakota. "Delicious! Is that what you just said?" Dakota teased and poked Bailey in her side. They chuckled.

"He ordered a bottle of this wine, amazing wine. It was called Opus one."

Dakota interjected once again, wide eyed. "Opus one! That's at least two hundred dollars a bottle! Did you know that?" she asked, sitting up straighter in bed.

"No way, it can't be!" Bailey choked.

"Oh, yes it is! Anyway, did you kiss him?" Dakota asked enthusiastically.

"I'm not telling. In any case, I'm tired. I'm going to bed. We can resume this conversation tomorrow. Rest. Remember, you're supposed to be sick. I'll see you for breakfast. Bye."

Bailey stood up and took two steps toward the door. As she turned the doorknob, she stopped, looked back to Dakota with her head slightly toward her and said, "He was nice."

She stepped into the hallway. As she shut the door behind her, heard Dakota yell, "You kissed him! We'll talk tomorrow." Bailey smiled on her way to her cabin.

***

Bailey was about to leave her room to meet Dakota for a day of shopping and sightseeing when there was a knock at her door.

"Who is it?" she asked. She approached the door to listen for an answer.

"Flowers for you, Miss Winters," the steward said. With a frown on her face, she opened the door.

"These came for you this morning, miss," he said and extended the vase toward her.

"I'm sorry, but I think you have the wrong person," she told him, taking a step back.

"Are you Bailey Winters?" he asked, standing in the hallway with the roses.

"Yes," Bailey answered, a little confused. *Who would send me flowers?* The steward handed her the roses and wished her a good day. She closed the door with her foot and set the vase on the small desk. She found the small envelope and pulled out the card. "Thanks for a lovely evening, Logan." She brought her hand to her heart and leaned forward to smell the roses.

"Gee, I wonder what I'd get after a second date," she said out loud. Unfortunately she didn't even know where to find him. He was just a passing ship in the night. How ironic!

She met Dakota in the lobby of the ship. They had an excursion planned for the day. They were both dressed in shorts, t-shirt, and sneakers. Bailey had brought a straw hat along to protect her from the sun.

"What took you so long? I thought you might have gotten lost. Ready for some shopping?" Dakota asked as Bailey walked toward her. Dakota jumped off her seat, grabbed her pocketbook and stood up.

"You are not going to believe why I was late," Bailey told her in a low voice.

"What happened?" Dakota asked.

"I was about to leave when two dozen roses were delivered to my cabin," she answered to Dakota with widened eyes. "They were from Logan."

"Girl, what did you do to deserve that? Shoot! I never get flowers after my first dates." They both laughed and hurried toward the gangway of the ship to board the bus that would take them to Pelican Village. Pelican Village was a small town, with colorful cottages that housed an amazing collection of the local arts and crafts stores of Barbados.

"Look how pretty it is! I bet we can find all kind of treasures!" Bailey told Dakota as they disembarked from the bus. They walked the short distance to the path leading to the stores. Dakota's eyes darted from right to left, looking at all the items displayed on the sidewalks.

"Where shall we begin?" Dakota asked. She took an area map out of her shoulder bag.

"Let's go this way first, and we can backtrack the opposite way," she said, pointing to the left.

"Okay, that's a start," Bailey answered. Dakota folded her map and stuck it in her shorts pocket. They went from store to store for hours, acquiring trinkets for their friends back home.

"Look over there, I see a little restaurant. Let's go get a cold drink and maybe a quick bite to eat. What do you think?" Dakota asked, as Bailey examined scarves on a rack. Bailey raised her arm to take a quick look at her watch. It was already three o'clock in the afternoon, and they had not eaten yet.

"Sure. I'm kind of thirsty and hungry," Bailey answered. They made their way to the pathway once again. As the girls approached the tiny bar and restaurant, Dakota lightly poked Bailey in the side with her elbow.

"What?" Bailey asked, surprised. Still walking, she turned to look at Dakota, wondering why she had poked her.

"Look over there," Dakota told her, eyeing a man with folded arms leaning against the door frame of the bar. He grinned their way, his eyes dancing. He stood erect as if he had been waiting for them. Bailey almost dropped her bags. She stared at the man, who was only about fifteen yards away from them. A smile crossed her lips. She continued to walk toward the entrance. She watched as he lifted his hand to wave their way.

"Oh God!" Bailey whispered to Dakota. Dakota didn't hear; she forged ahead straight for him, while Bailey trailed behind her.

"Hey! How are you?" she heard him say. Logan's long blond curls were blowing in the wind. He was casually dressed in a neon t-shirt and cut offs with sandals. Why did she think he looked sexy, even though she would never before have given a man dressed that way a second look?

"Fine, and you?" was all Bailey could say. But Dakota was not without words.

"Hi, nice to see you again. We were just about to get a bite to eat and get a cold drink," Dakota said. She pushed her way past him into the tiny place. It only held a half dozen plastic tables and chairs, and a bamboo bar area. Bailey stood facing him, holding her bags by her side. She finally gazed up at him. He seemed to be waiting for her to speak, his eyes focused on her lips. He leaned forward and gave her a peck on her cheek. She felt his soft lips brush her cheek. Her heart skipped a beat at the kiss, and seeing him standing in front of her. He pulled back and said, "Let me help you with your bags." All she could do was let go of them when he grasped them in his hands.

"Thank you so much for the flowers," she managed to say. She was happy to see him again.

"You're welcome. I had a good time last night." She walked in front of him to the table where Dakota was sitting, pulled out a chair, and sat down. Bailey glanced at Dakota and gave her a small smile. Logan gently placed the bags on another chair near Bailey, and took the empty chair next to her. Bailey laced her fingers on her lap and looked around the restaurant for the server. She desperately wanted something, anything, to drink. She was nervous.

"What a coincidence to meet you here. By the way, I ordered three frozen drinks, Miami Vice. I hope that was all right?" Dakota asked, opening her menu. Bailey nodded her way.

"I was in the area when I spotted you. I'm not disappointed, seeing you again," Logan said, with eyes locked on Bailey.

"How are you feeling, Dakota? Bailey told me you were sick last night," he asked. He slowly turned his face toward Dakota. Bailey grabbed her menu but, again, she couldn't concentrate on the list of dishes. She suddenly felt Logan's knee rub against hers. She froze and was unable to pull her leg away. He felt so warm against her skin.

"I'm just fine. Nothing to worry about. What do you suggest?" Dakota asked as the waiter placed their drinks in front of them. Bailey took a sip.

"The pork sandwich or the salads are the best," Logan answered, handing his menu to the server.

"I'll take the salad," Bailey said as she tried to regain her senses. She had not expected to see Logan again, but she was pleased.

"So tell me, how are you enjoying your cruise? What island is next?" Logan inquired.

"We're having a blast, and it's very relaxing. We're leaving here this evening, and we'll be docking in St. Lucia tomorrow morning," Bailey said. She'd finally found her voice. They chatted about their plans for the next week. The sun was going down and they were still sitting and talking in the restaurant. Bailey was on her third drink and was feeling tipsy. She giggled at Logan's jokes and felt more comfortable. She swallowed the last drop of her drink and placed the glass on the table.

"I think I've had enough. The last bus will be leaving soon. I'm heading back to the ship, but please stay, Bailey. You have a few hours before we sail," Dakota said as she stood. She bent down and picked up her pocketbook and her bags. Bailey smiled at Logan, pushing her chair back to leave, when she felt his hand on top of hers to stop her. She glanced at him.

"I'll drive you back to the ship later, if you'll allow me. I want to show you something special," he said, then smiled. Her mouth opened, but no words came out. She couldn't leave Dakota by herself again or could she? But before she could move, she heard Dakota say, "That's perfect. Why should you leave because I'm tired? I'll see you onboard," Dakota said with a nod.

"Dakota, I don't want you to..." Bailey was interrupted by Logan's suggestion.

"We'll walk you back to the bus. That way you won't worry, and my ride is in the parking area, too. Okay?" He tapped Bailey's hand gently, then pushed his chair back and stood.

"That's not necessary. I'm a big girl, I can find my way," Dakota said.

"I insist. Otherwise, I'm going back with you," Bailey told her firmly as she picked up her bags.

"All right, let's go," Dakota answered. They exited the restaurant and were on the walkway headed back to the ship when Bailey felt

Logan's hand touch hers. She gasped a little as his fingers intertwined with hers. She turned her head to look at him. He tilted his head toward her as he squeezed her hand a bit. She smiled.

Bailey waved goodbye as the bus rolled down the street on its way back to the ship.

"So, what did you want to show me?" Bailey asked. They stood side by side in the parking lot, his hand on the small of her back.

"First..." He pulled her against his hard body, his hands caressing her back. She looked up at him as he bent his head down, and his lips came crashing upon hers. She closed her eyes and kissed him back. She felt the heat of his body against hers, bringing a hot sensation down to her core; something she'd thought would never happen again after her last break-up. His tongue tasted like mint as it explored hers. He pulled back and nipped at her lips. She licked her lips, wanting more.

"I've wanted to do that since I met you last night," he whispered. She felt his mouth near her ear and he gently bit her earlobe. Her heart was pounding hard against her chest. She heard a moan. Stunned, she realized it came from her.

He took a step backward, keeping her at arms' length, and grinned at her. She could feel the heat rising up to her face, but she didn't care. She brought her hand to her mouth as she giggled out loud.

"Sorry, it's been awhile since someone kissed me like that," she tried to explain as she bowed her head. He pulled her close.

"I think it's kind of sexy when a woman moans," he said. She locked eyes on him and smiled. She slipped her hand around his toned waist, his hip touching hers as they walked in the parking lot.

"Let's go for a ride." He pointed to a Harley motorcycle, parked on his left. He let go of her to unlock the helmets that were secured to the backseat. He turned toward her with one helmet in his hand. She just stood there, hands by her side, watching him.

"That's your ride? I've never ridden a bike before. I'm not sure if..." She could feel her legs starting to tremble at the prospect of mounting the bike.

"I promise I won't drive fast, and all you have to do is hold on to me. I'll be careful," he reassured her. She nodded at him, but did not move an inch. He raised the helmet and placed it on her head, and fastened the strap for her.

"Don't be afraid. I'm a good driver. Let's go sightseeing," he said. He rubbed her arms to relax her.

"Okay," she managed to murmur. *What am I getting into? I really hope he's a good driver. You wanted something different. Well, here's your chance.* She watched him put his helmet on, straddle the bike, and grip the handlebars.

"Ready? Let's go," he said, extending one hand to her. She took a couple of steps closer. She placed her right palm on his shoulder and raised her leg up and over the bike. She sat down behind him.

"Wrap your arms around my torso," he instructed her. He took her hand and positioned it on his hard stomach. She could feel the ripples of his muscles. She scooted forward until her breasts were pressing hard against his back and her legs surrounded his. She liked the closeness she felt, nestled against him. She inhaled deeply, then let it go. She heard the motor roar as she tighten her grip around him. He stroked up and down on her upper leg to reassure her. His touch brought a burning sensation down to her center.

The bike moved forward down the street, the warm wind of the island enveloping them. She leaned her chin on his shoulder, her muscles relaxing, but she wouldn't let go.

"I like it, I'm not afraid," she yelled near his ear. He just nodded his head.

They rode up and down the streets of Bridgetown for about an hour, admiring the sights of the town. She could see the pier from a distance. They passed several small villages and green open fields. The hours flew by like minutes.

She felt a lump in her throat when the motorcycle parked near the gangway of her ship. She didn't want this feeling to end. She slowly pulled her arms back as she disembarked from the bike. Within seconds he'd shut off the engine and the motorbike was on its stand. He helped her remove her helmet, took off his own, and secured them to the back of the bike. He turned toward her, placed his hands on her hips and pulled her close. Her face was inches from his. She knew this was going to be their last kiss. His palms cupped her face in his hands. She could feel his thumbs stroking her cheeks. His eyes pierced her defenses as his mouth came crashing down, their tongues dancing in the perfect rhythm. Her arms held him tightly as she felt his erection mounting, rubbing against her body. He finally pulled back, his hands still enveloping her face.

"You're so beautiful, but if I don't stop now, I might not let you go," he told her in a low voice. *I wish I didn't have to go either*, she thought. He let go of her.

"Well, thank you for everything. It was fun," she said. He pushed a few stray strands of her hair away from her face. She brushed his hand with the tips of her fingers.

"I'll see you soon. Now go, before you miss the ship," he told her. *Yeah, right! I'm sure*, she thought. Her heart felt heavy. She didn't want to leave him. What was this? A fling? He was from the islands and he probably had many girlfriends. Bailey commanded her legs to walk toward the entrance of the ship's gangway. She didn't look back as she stepped onto the narrow bridge, but she had to have one last look to engrave today into her mind. She turned around and saw him, with his helmet on, sitting on his Harley. She waved goodbye as she heard the roar of the engine and he rode away. Her eyes teared up a little because maybe, just maybe, it could have been something special if they'd had more time—and did not come from two different worlds.

CHAPTER 4

About thirty minutes later, Logan was back on *The Vagabond* and standing on the part of the stern with a view of Bailey's cruise ship. He leaned against the railing with a whiskey in one hand, watching the ship depart the Bridgetown port. He gulped down his drink. A grimace appeared on his face; not from the alcohol, but due to Bailey leaving. He thought back to their last kiss and how he wanted to keep her by his side. He wanted to make love to her. *Her body fit perfectly against his back when they were riding around the island!* It had given him a sense of contentment and, more importantly, a feeling of being desired without her knowing much about him or his money.

For the first time in years, he yearned to have a woman by his side to share his life! He didn't just want one night. He wanted Bailey. She was uncomplicated and modest. He could still hear her giggles; they warmed him all over. In the past two days, he'd felt excitement and real joy in his life again—something his fortune couldn't buy. He bowed his head as numbness from the alcohol invaded him. He gripped the steel railing and held it tight.

His reflections of Bailey were disturbed when he heard footsteps behind him. He lifted his head, but did not turn to face the person approaching. He already knew it was Henry.

"Do you need anything else this evening, sir?" Henry asked politely, and waited for an answer from his employer. Henry routinely did this, every night before he retired downstairs. Logan looked out at the clear water in the darkness; he took a long breath in and out, but did not budge from his spot.

"Henry, do you believe in love at first sight?" he asked his longtime friend, hoping for direction. Henry was quiet for a moment before he spoke again.

"Yes, sir, I believe it can happen," the wise man said. Logan turned and looked at him. Henry was standing erect, his hands clasped behind his back. A feeling of hope and joy invaded Logan's mind. He debated what to do.

"Could you inform Captain Ryan I have a new course, please? I want to head to St. Lucia immediately. That will be all," he told Henry. Logan saw the corners of Henry's mouth lift into a smile. He said, "Very good sir, I shall tell him right away,"

Henry took a step forward toward the stairway to the bridge when Logan said, "Thank you, Henry."

Henry paused to glance his way. "You are most welcome, sir," he replied. He nodded at Logan, and resumed his pace to give the Captain the new course.

***

Logan was in bed, sleeping in his stateroom as the sun rose, when he heard a knock on his cabin door.

"Sir, it's Henry, may I enter?" Logan stirred in his bed and opened his eyes.

"Yes, Henry, come in," he answered. The door opened smoothly. Henry came forward and closed the door behind him. He was holding a cup of coffee in his left hand, and placed it on the side table next to Logan's bed with an envelope.

"Good morning, sir," Henry said joyfully.

Logan stretched his arms trying to wake up. "Morning, Henry," he mumbled, still half asleep.

"We are docked at Port of Castries. Miss Bailey's ship is also docked nearby. I took the liberty of inquiring where she might be going today. She will be snorkeling near Marigot Bay. Her friend will not accompany her today, she will be scuba diving. I acquired directions for the snorkeling location, and rented a catamaran for you. I hope you don't mind?" Henry asked. He walked over and opened the window shades before turning toward Logan.

Logan pushed himself up into a sitting position, leaning his head against the fabric headboard. Logan snickered as he reached over for the steaming beverage and took a sip.

"Henry, have I ever told you how much I appreciate all your snooping?" Logan asked. He smiled, thinking he couldn't wait to see Bailey again.

"Sir, the excursion will be taking off in about an hour, from the main pier. May I suggest you take a quick shower and get going? I also told the deckhands to prepare your motorbike," Henry informed Logan. He walked to the door and waited.

"You are the best, thank you," Logan said. He pushed the covers off himself to the other side of the bed and hurriedly walked to the bathroom to get ready. Forty-five minutes later he was parked next to the excursion bus, waiting patiently for Bailey to appear. His eyes were glued to the gangway as he watched every passenger disembark. His heart was beating a little fast in anticipation of seeing her again. Logan was dressed all in black, his helmet resting between his legs on the gas tank and arms folded in front of him. He waited patiently—at least it looked that way. His excitement was difficult to conceal.

There she was, chatting with other passengers, dressed in beige shorts and a blue tank top. He could see the straps of her bathing suit tied to the back of her neck. She was carrying a beach backpack on her shoulder. When she was about twenty feet from the bus she abruptly stopped walking. Her mouth dropped open in surprise. A smile crossed her face. She excused herself from the other people and headed toward him.

"Hi, gorgeous," Logan said, with a grin on his face.

"How did you...What are you doing here?" she asked, confused.

"I came to take you snorkeling. Are you ready?" he asked. He unhooked the spare helmet and offered it to her. She turned her head and pointed toward the bus, but no sound came out of her mouth. She slowly took the helmet in her hand and stared at him.

"Okay...Just let me tell the deckhand I won't be going on the bus," she said. She walked over to inform him of her change of plans, then sauntered back to Logan.

"Are you following me?" she asked with a nervous giggle. He could see she needed answers for his being there. She shifted her weight from one leg to the other and adjusted her backpack.

"Yes, I am. I was hoping to get to know you a little better. I own a boat, remember? I wanted to spend more time with you, so I sailed here. I hope you don't mind," he told her. She seemed to relax a little as she looked down at the helmet in her hand. She seemed to be considering if she should come or not.

"I won't hurt you. I just want to spend more time with you," he assured her as he extended his hand to her. With her eyes locked on his, she nodded. She put her helmet on as he pulled his buttocks forward so she could sit behind him. She lifted her leg and straddled the back of the motorbike. The same sexual feeling passed through him as last night, when he felt her body hug his and her arms enfold his torso. It felt great to have a woman's arms around him.

"So, where are we going?" she yelled as his bike started rolling down the pier.

"We are going snorkeling, I rented a catamaran. It's parked at the other end of the dock," he shouted back, trying to concentrate on his driving and not the returning lust he felt between his legs for her.

***

Bailey cuddled close against Logan's back, still feeling shocked that he'd traveled to St. Lucia just so he could spend more time with her. *What did this man really do for a job that allowed him to afford expensive bottles of wine and sailing around the Caribbean Islands at the blink of an eye? Real estate was what he told me, but so what?! Be adventurous! You only live once, right? Well, he must be selling skyscrapers!* She sniggered out loud at the thought and for right now she was happy just to have his company and to hold him near.

"What is so funny? I can hear you," he shouted as they continued to ride down the dock.

"Nothing, nothing, I'll tell you later," she answered. She squeezed him tighter against her belly. She admired the island's green mountaintops as he swerved along them and she could see the glistening, calm, blue sea from afar. *Where was he taking her?*

He turned into a long, narrow parking lot on the east side of the dock and shut the bike off. She dismounted while he held the bike steady for her. He jumped off the bike, and she watched him intently as he locked up the helmets. He opened the left saddlebag and took out a canvas bag.

"I brought a few things for lunch, that is if you get hungry," he said as he slipped his arm around her upper body and pulled her against his chest. She was hungry all right, but not for food. He bent over and kissed her on the lips. He let go of her and grabbed her right hand to lead the way down the wooden pier.

"Ready? Let's go." They stopped at the end of the dock in front of a twenty-five foot catamaran.

"After you." He bowed as if she were his princess and extended his hand. They boarded the boat, and she sat down in one of the seats. The boat was very clean, with green-cushioned seats on two sides with a table in the middle. There was a sunbathing area in the front, and she could see a bathroom down to her left. There was a small bridge area to the side where the controls and the steering wheel were, with one white leather seat.

She watched as he sat down in the captain's seat and turned on the engine. He grasped the helm and slowly navigated toward the open waters. She sat quietly, just admiring the view of the island, with the beautiful backdrop of the Pitons in the mountainous region. When they were halfway out, he took his T-shirt off and threw it to the side. She ogled his muscular shoulders and his washboard abdominal area. He turned a knob and the sounds of Caribbean music played in the background. She tapped her feet on the deck and bobbed her head to the rhythm of the music. He glanced her way, but didn't say a word. He just smiled broadly at her and continued to steer the boat.

"I love the tunes. I hope you know where we're going, and what you're doing, because I'm clueless," she joked. She stood up and danced her way to him. His eyes were on the blue waters so she wrapped her arms around his shoulders and laid her hands on his chest. She leaned down to kiss him on the side of the neck, and then his earlobe. He tilted his head and touched her hand. She glided her fingers near his nipples on his chest. *I just want to rub my hand all the way down past his belly button and...Stop thinking that way you little witch. Just take your time. You don't want him to think you're easy prey.*

"Mmm. You better not do that while I'm driving, it could be dangerous. I might crash," he teased her.

"Ha, ha! Very well, then. I'll just lay down here and sunbathe until we arrive at our destination," she said.

Bailey proceeded to unbutton her shorts and let them drop to the floor as she danced around the deck. She pulled her shirt over her head, showing off her blue and pink bikini. She took her towel out of her bag and spread it on the back deck. She sat down and took out a bottle of sunscreen. She had just rubbed lotion down her legs, arms, and torso when she heard the engine shut off. She looked toward him and he was sitting back in his seat with his arm over the back of the seat. He had a sexy grin across his face.

"Need any help?" he asked as he eyed her body from head to toe.

"Maybe..." she giggled as she bit her lower lip gently.

"Would you like me to apply some lotion on your back?" he asked.

"Sure." She handed the bottle to him and he stepped forward, grabbed it, and squirted some lotion in his hand. She turned over on her belly, her arms under her chin, and waited impatiently for his touch. His soft hands coasted down her back down to her buttocks. The tips of his fingers massaged her just under her bathing suit bottom and down the back of her legs. She closed her eyes, enjoying every stroke of his hand.

"Feels good," she said in a trembling voice. Bailey was trying not to lose control of her desire for this man. She hadn't been attracted to anyone since her break-up. She was unsure and afraid of being hurt again. She didn't want only a sexual relationship with this man. She wanted to get to know him before she got involved with him. *Who do you think you're fooling? Here you are sunbathing in the middle of nowhere, alone with a man you just met two day ago, and all you can think about is what your ex-boyfriend did to you. You're crazy.*

"I need to cool off," she heard Logan say. Then she heard a huge splash from the side of the boat. She opened her eyes, startled and looked in the direction of the noise. She rose to her feet and ran to the side of the boat. She saw Logan swimming in the clear aqua water. He resurfaced about thirty feet away, wiping back the salt water from his face and pushing his hair back with his hands. His wet body glistened in the sunlight.

"Come on, jump!" he yelled as he swam closer to the side of the boat.

"All right, here I come," she said. Bailey swung her legs over the edge and sat with her feet in the water. She leaned and pushed forward. The water was colder than she thought it would be, but within seconds she popped up to the surface. She felt Logan's hands around her midsection. She treaded water with her feet to stay afloat and placed her hands around his shoulders. She could feel the heat of his body against hers, even though the water was cool. His lips were inches from hers. She leaned forward and kissed him hard. She had to pull away from him because she couldn't breathe, and the water was up to her neck. She felt his hands slide from her body. She looked at him and said, "I think if I continue this kiss I might drown." They both laughed together.

"I'll get the snorkeling gear and we will enjoy the fish for a while," Logan suggested. She swam with him to the ladder at the back of the boat. She braced her hand on the railing of the ladder for support as she watched him mount the steps to the catamaran.

"Are there a lot of different species here, and how big are they?" she asked as he went inside the cabin to fetch their gear.

Returning with the gear, he answered, "Well, it doesn't look too deep here so we will hopefully see a lot by the reef over there." He handed her a snorkel mask and fins. She watched him drop back into the water as they both rinsed their masks and adjusted them on their heads. He helped her put on her fins.

"Ready?" he asked. She nodded. He took her hand. They floated and paddled in the water. She felt a closeness she couldn't deny.

Two hours later they were back on the deck, dripping wet. They both dried off with big, fluffy towels. Bailey wrapped her towel around her hips and sat down on one of the cushions on the deck.

"That was so much fun. I've never seen so many varieties of fish," she said, delighted. She took out her hairbrush from her beach bag and combed her long black hair.

"Are you thirsty? I brought water, but if you want I can open this," he said. He pulled out a bottle of red wine from his canvas bag.

"I'll have both. First, I'll take the water; then the wine. What else do you have in that goody bag?" she asked as she looked up at him. He walked over and sat next to her on her cushion. He handed the bottle of water to her and she gulped it down. He spread out a small towel and prepared a spread of Gouda cheese, grapes, a French baguette, cold chicken breast, and a knife.

She watched in amazement at all he had taken out.

"What else do you have in that bag? Did you prepare all this?" He didn't answer her right away. Instead, he gave her a smirk as he pulled out the wine cork.

"To tell you the truth, no. A friend of mine helped," he admitted.

He poured two glasses of wine, handed one to her and said, "A toast! May we have many more days like today."

"I'll drink to that, and thank you for taking me away," she told him. They both took sips of their wine. He leaned over and gave her a peck on the mouth.

"Let's eat, I'm starving," he said and patted his stomach.

"Yes, I can hear your stomach groan," she said and they both laughed.

***

The afternoon flew by and before they knew it, the sun was setting over the horizon. Bailey leaned against Logan's shoulder, his left arm wrapped around her. They both gazed at the sunset over the water.

Logan had held Bailey near him all afternoon. They talked about their lives, aspirations, travels and hobbies. The only thing Logan did not mention to her was how wealthy he was. With every passing minute, Logan's feelings for her grew stronger and stronger. How could he feel such a strong attraction to someone he hardly knew?

"The orange combined with the yellow is what I love to see the most of the sunset from my boat," he said. He noticed that Bailey did not answer. He looked downward to see why she was so quiet. He bent over and kissed the top of her head; she was snoozing. She seemed to be an angel sent to him by God to overcome his loneliness.

They'd had a long day and she must be tired, so he let her sleep. He picked up the dry towel next to him and covered her shoulders. He had a feeling of peace and contentment with her near him. He wondered if she felt the same. He closed his eyes and soaked in the last few rays of the sun. The boat rocked with the light waves and Logan fell asleep with Bailey in his arms.

***

"Logan, wake up!" Her panicked voice echoed as she shook his arm. He opened his eyes wide and looked at her, startled. Fright was written starkly on her face and darkness was upon them.

"Are you okay? What's the matter?" He sat upright. She grabbed her shorts and her shirt and frantically put them on. She raised her wrist and glanced at her watch.

"We have to get back right away. We overslept. The cruise ship will be leaving in half hour. Oh my God, we aren't going to make it, are we? What am I going to do?" she asked him, tears pooling in her eyes. He stood up and in two long strides was at the controls. He turned the key to start the engine and steered the boat back toward the shore. He turned his head to glance back at her. She was pacing back and forth from each sides of the boat.

"Bailey. Bailey!" he shouted at her. She stopped walking and faced him. He saw tears falling down her cheeks. This broke his heart.

"Come here," as he extended his hand to her. She came near him and he pulled her close in an embrace.

40

"What am I going to do if the ship leaves without me? How am I going to get ahold of Dakota? She will be so worried." Bailey wept, both her hands coming up to cover her face.

"Bailey, I'm so sorry, but please stop crying. It will be fine," he said. Logan tried to console her by rubbing her arm and holding her near. Logan knew they would probably not make the ship, but he was fine with that. He would get to spend more time with her.

"Listen to me," he told her as her watery eyes peered at him. He smiled at her.

"Don't worry. I'll take care of everything. I just want you to stop sobbing, please," he pleaded with her.

"How are you going to do that? I don't have my credit cards, my passport...Oh, God." She turned away from him and went to sit on one of the benches. At least she had stopped crying.

"Bailey, do you trust me?" He yelled above the sound of the waves. She looked at him and finally nodded slightly.

"I'll take care of it, do you understand? Trust me,'" he shouted. She just sat quietly as the boat headed back toward the island. Logan continued to steer the catamaran in silence. If the cruise ship wasn't at the dock, there was no way he'd be able to keep his secret. She would see the yacht. *I won't lie to her about it.* He could see the lights of the dock as he approached the marina. He scanned the area for her cruise ship. He could see the larger ones, but Bailey's ship was nowhere to be seen. It had departed without her. She was now standing near him as he glided into an empty spot and moored the boat to the quay.

When she didn't see the ship she said, sadly, "It's gone." She bowed and shook her head. She picked up her bag, swung it over her shoulder, and walked to his bike. No tears fell, but he knew she was worried. When he arrived at his motorbike he wrapped his arms around her and pulled her close. She didn't resist, but he saw her eyes pool once again. He lifted her chin with one hand so he could see her face.

"Bailey, I'm really sorry for what happened. I will fix it. We'll contact Dakota and tell her you're safe. Then I'll take you to your next cruise destination, okay?"

She frowned at him as tears started to fall again. His heart broke to see her so unhappy.

"It's not all your fault, I fell asleep, too. I might have to borrow some money from you until I can get back," she whispered, as he hugged her against his chest. He could feel his shirt getting wet. He couldn't bear to see her miserable any more. He pushed her away from him, to arm's length. He held on to her arm and turned her around, toward the opposite direction of the pier.

"Do you see that yacht over there? The one that's all lit up with the white lights?" he asked, pointing to his ship. She nodded, but not a sound came out of her.

"That's *The Vagabond*. We are going to board it in a few minutes and go join Dakota," he said.

She turned white and looked at him with a confused expression.

"Sure we are. Are you crazy?" She laughed nervously and took a step away from him.

"Where are you going?" he asked as she backed away from him.

"I am not going to do anything illegal, like board that yacht!" she snapped at him. She started to walk away from him.

"It's my yacht," he told her.

She stopped walking, whipped around to look at him and said, "What?"

He nodded and grinned.

"Oh! My God, that's yours?" she asked and started to laugh again hysterically.

"You told me you had a boat, not a yacht," she said. Her mouth opened in shock and her eyes widened.

"You never asked how big my boat was, did you? Come on. Let's go find your cruise ship," he extended his hand to her. Bailey frowned at him like she was unsure, but slowly placed her hand in his. She smiled, and he pulled her against his chest once again.

"Now do you understand? I told you I would fix it."

She wrapped her arms around him and lifted up on her toes to kiss him. He held her tight as their tongues swayed together. A shudder raced down his spine. He wanted her. He yearned to make love to her. His sexual desires increased as he held her, but he knew that now was not the time. He pulled away.

"Ready?" he asked. He reached into his pocket for his cell phone and dialed Henry.

"Good evening, Henry. Could you advise Captain Cooper to prepare to set sail? I'll be there shortly to give him the destination." He listened for a moment, then hung up the phone.

"We're all set." They mounted the motorcycle. She pressed her body close behind him, and they headed toward his yacht.

CHAPTER 5

B ailey was in awe; she wore an expression of disbelief as they approached the ship. She noticed two men in blue shorts and white shirts on the pier next to the yacht. Both were standing with their hands behind their backs, waiting for them to arrive. Logan drove his Harley down the wharf to the entrance of the ship. The younger man assisted Logan with the bike as soon as he turned off the engine. Bailey dismounted and removed her helmet. Logan placed both helmets on seat of the bike.

"Thank you Michael, you can take it. I won't need it again," Logan said. The deckhand rolled the bike away.

Baily felt Logan slip his hand into hers. "Bailey, I'd like you to meet my personal assistant and good friend, Henry," he said.

Henry extended his hand to her. She shook it and said, "Nice to meet you Henry," with a smiled glued to her face.

"The pleasure is all mine," he replied and cast a look toward Logan. She saw a slight nod from Henry.

"Henry, could try to send a message to the Windstar Cruise ship and ask what their heading is? Tell them Bailey Winters will be joining them at their next destination. Also, advise Dakota..." he glanced at Bailey.

"Rogers," she answered.

"...Dakota Rogers that Bailey is in good hands. Could you check with the captain pertaining to her passport? They have it onboard."

"Very well, sir. Anything else?" Henry asked as they boarded the ship.

"Could you have John throw us something together to eat? We'll be on the sun deck. Thank you."

Logan slipped his hand behind her back and said, "Come on, I'll show you around." She was speechless, and could only nod. He led the way up the gateway to the ship. She followed him closely as they walked to the inside of the boat, up a spiral stairway, and out to a massive sundeck that was located near the stern. Her legs were trembling from excitement with every step she took. She needed to sit down. She spotted a bar area and reached for the stool and sat down.

She examined the teak deck, equipped with a large sun pads surrounding the Jacuzzi. She could see a living room area in the background, decorated with white furnishings. Just beyond was a small dining area. *Who the hell is this man that he can afford to live here?* she asked herself. She placed her hands on the counter and tried to get her senses again. She could feel her heart beating, fast against her chest. She needed to calm down.

"I'll give you a tour after we eat. What would you like to drink?" he asked. She watched Logan move to the back of the bar. Still unable to speak from the shock of it all, she murmured, "Whatever you're having is fine."

"Vodka on the rocks okay?" he asked.

"Make it a double," she answered.

Logan laughed as he took two tumblers, added ice and poured Grey Goose vodka into them. He set one in front of her. She noticed that her hand was trembling as she raised the glass to her mouth. She quickly took a large mouthful. She felt it burn going down; it sure woke her up, and brought her back to reality. She scowled. She glanced up at him, and he was watching her every move. He took a sip of his drink.

"Any more surprises that I don't know about before we sail?" she asked him. She took another sip.

"Not really," he answered. Logan refilled her glass.

"Let's sit over there. It's more comfortable, and we'll be able to see the harbor lights when we leave the port," he suggested. He walked around and offered his hand to her. She could feel the alcohol taking effect. She felt calmer and her legs were sturdier when she stood. Her heartbeat was back to normal. She took his hand and he escorted her to sit down next to him on the cushions. She felt the slight vibration of the moving boat. Logan was quiet for a few minutes. He wrapped his arm around her shoulders and his fingers played with her hair in the darkness of the night. His touch was so soft.

Still in amazement, Bailey asked in a very serious tone, "Why didn't you tell me about all of this? Did you think I'd take advantage of you?" She kept her sight straight ahead.

"What was I supposed to say? I live on a yacht and don't need to work. I was trying to find someone who would like me. Not my money, but me," he said. His voice seemed to have trailed off into a whisper. He turned and looked away. She bowed her head for an instant, feeling regretful that she had spoken to him so harshly. His hand had stopped moving. It was now resting on the back of their seat.

"I would have liked you with or without money. I'm not like that. I judge a person by how they treat the other people," she said. She placed her drink down on the table in front of her. She touched his chin gently and moved his face toward her so she could look into his sapphire eyes.

"I like you just as you are," she whispered and kissed him on the lips. She could feel his arm tighten around her shoulder. He pulled her against his chest. She kissed him sweetly, and placed her head on his shoulder.

"I like you too." They held on to each other. He stroked her back with his fingertips. His touches were like shockwaves, igniting her sexual desires. She wondered what it would be like to take him to bed; to be able to caress his body and feel him inside her. Her thoughts were interrupted when they heard someone step upon the deck. She turned to see the steward bringing a large tray of sushi and lobster. He delivered it and left the area without a word.

Logan said, "I hope you like sushi. If not I can have them get something else, like..."

"I love sushi," she interrupted.

Logan flirted with her as he fed her tuna, licked her fingers when she fed him. He was very attentive to her needs. Bailey found herself wondering if she could take a chance with him. *Will he hurt me like my last boyfriend?*

Time passed quickly. They ate and talked; she learned a lot within a few hours. He was simple man and humble. He wasn't a spoiled brat. He must have a lot of women after him. A streak of jealousy invaded her just thinking about it.

He interrupted her thoughts when he placed his hand on her knee.

"Are you enjoying yourself? Is there anything I can get for you? You okay?" he asked as he caressed her leg.

"Oh! Yes, I was just thinking about Dakota. I'm happy just sitting with you by my side," she answered and squeezed his hand gently.

They relaxed with an after dinner cognac and watched the lights disappear from the horizon. He gave her a tour of the ship and she found every room to be luxurious. There was a chandelier in the main stateroom, a full kitchen, lots of bathrooms, and plenty of water toys to amuse anyone. It even had a helicopter pad. Impressive! She was amazed. *How much did this yacht cost?* She didn't dare ask the question. He must be extremely wealthy to afford luxuries like this, but she didn't care. She just wanted to find a man she could trust; one who would be loyal to her.

It was getting late and her eyelids were feeling heavy. She didn't want to sleep, she enjoyed talking and cuddling so much.

"I know you're tired. It's late, let me show you to your room. We have all day tomorrow to chat," Logan said. He took her hand and led her to her room. They descended the stairway to her room. Suddenly, she was wide-awake. She stopped walking in the hallway in front of his room. She looked up at him, slipped her arm around his torso and brought him close to her until their hips were together. She whispered, "I don't want to sleep alone tonight."

He stared into her eyes. He smiled a sexy grin. His mouth crashed down on hers. She could feel him growing against her. She reached up and stroked her fingers through his blond curls. His hand slipped under her shirt to massage the bare skin of her back.

A shiver made her body tremble. She wanted him. He opened the door to his room and pushed her backwards, through the archway of his stateroom.

"Are you sure you want to...?" He didn't have time to finish his sentence.

She placed her index finger on his mouth. "Shhhh! I'm sure. I want to be with the man I first met at the bar with the blue eyes," she answered.

She took two paces back and entered his stateroom pulling, him toward her until her body was against hers. She put her arms around his neck and kissed him passionately. Logan held her close and lifted her off her feet. He kicked the door shut with his foot and started to undress her. He spread his delicate kisses on her upper body until his embrace made her legs weak. He gently picked her up and carried her to his king-size bed. He moved his body on top of hers. His moist lips kissed her neck and his tongue slid down her neck to nibble on her breasts.

***

Bailey woke up to the slow, undulating movement of the ship. It was early morning. She felt an arm swaddling her waist with a sheet. She could feel Logan's warm breath against her neck. She opened her eyes and touched his hand with her fingertips. She closed her eyes and inhaled the scent of their lovemaking. It was all over her body. She reminisced about the night they had just spent together. She slowly took his hand in hers, lifted it off her body, and carefully placed it on the bed as she slipped out of it.

She tiptoed to his closet and opened it quietly. She scanned his clothes, trying to find something to wear. She unhooked a blue linen shirt. The shirt went down to her knees; a little big, but it would do. She fastened the buttons one at a time, then turned toward the door. She walked on the balls of her feet, trying not to wake him. Bailey opened the door and reclosed it behind her silently. She walked to the end of the hall and stepped down the spiral staircase to the galley, the kitchen of the ship. As she entered, the chef lifted his head and looked at her with surprise, as did the two stewards who were standing there. She felt heat rise to her face.

"May I help you?" the chef asked. Bailey's mouth opened to speak, but she heard another man behind her speak.

"That's okay, Roger, I'll help Miss Bailey." She spun around and was face to face with Henry. He gently took her arm and pulled her aside.

"What can I do for you, Miss?" he asked with a smile. She bent her head down, embarrassed by being caught half-dressed. *I should have known better!* She twirled her fingers and said in a low voice, "I just wanted to get some coffee and fruit for Logan."

"That's no problem, Miss. If you want, I'll bring it up to you," Henry said. He gave her a wide smile. She felt the heat rise to her face again. *I must be beet red by now. I knew that he had a chef onboard!* Now she would have to tell Henry she was in Logan's stateroom.

"I'm not in...um..." She tried to explain, but he cut in and said, "I understand. Your secret is safe with me. I will bring it to Logan's room."

Bailey nervously played with her hair and said, "Thank you, Henry" What else could she say? She hurried up the stairs, taking them two at a time, to get back to the room. She quietly turned the knob, sneaked back into the room, and shut the door.

"Good morning, gorgeous. Where did you run off to?" Logan asked. He sat up in bed with half his body uncovered. She licked her lips at the sight of him.

"Well, I went to get coffee and fruit for you, but when I got to the kitchen..." Logan started to laugh out loud and extended his arms for her to come join him in bed. She suppressed a giggle as she went to sit beside him.

"It's not funny. I didn't expect to have a bunch of people in the kitchen stare at me in your shirt. I should have thought this over before I left, but I was saved by Henry." Logan was still chuckling. Bailey punched him lightly in the stomach. He grabbed her by the arms, threw her under him, and kissed her neck playfully.

"We'll just have to find you something else to wear," he told her, unbuttoning his shirt. He stopped when he heard a knock on his door. Bailey snatched the sheet up to cover her body when Logan said, "Come in, Henry."

Logan sat up in bed, but not without pulling Bailey against his chest. Henry entered and placed a tray with a pot of coffee and a platter of fruit on the side table. He stepped back with his arms by his side, looking only at Logan.

"Good morning, sir. Miss Bailey requested coffee and fruit. Will there be anything else?"

"No. Thank you, Henry, much appreciated," Logan answered. They watched him leave the room without another word. When the door closed, Logan snatched Bailey up in his arms.

"Now, where were we?" he teased. He started to cover her with kisses as one hand slid up her legs.

***

An hour later, they were sailing toward the island of St. George. Logan was pleased they were going to be at sea the whole day, and would not dock until the early hours of the morning. He stood under the spray of the shower letting the water flow down his body. He felt happy, and wondered if she would stay by his side or return to the Windstar tomorrow evening. He didn't want her to leave his side; he longed to know her every secret.

He loved how modest she was. Bailey wasn't like the women he usually met, who would throw themselves upon him hoping to get his attention or his fortune. She was considerate and beautiful, even this morning when she had ventured to the galley to get him coffee. He thought about how she had said she was saving money so she could buy a farm for a sanctuary to care for abandoned animals. He turned the knob to shut the water off, opened the glass door, stepped out and picked up a towel to dry himself. He wrapped it around his midriff and walked toward his closet, which was in his bedroom, to get dress. He poked his head into the salon area to check on Bailey.

Henry had delivered a pair of blue shorts and an oversized white polo jersey for Bailey to put on after bathing. She sat on the loveseat with her feet propped up on the corner of an ottoman, watching television and eating strawberries. *How innocent she looks!* Bailey had tied her hair into a messy bun, with soft strands of hair falling around her face.

Logan quickly slipped on a pair of faded cargo shorts and a t-shirt.

"Hey! Are you ready to go? I see you couldn't wait," he said. She stopped chewing her strawberry. She pursed her lips together as she lifted her eyes up to him, and smiled with a mouthful.

"I couldn't help myself. They looked so good. I don't know why I'm so hungry," she answered. She covered the dish with her hands so he wouldn't see she had almost eaten them all.

"I kept a few for you," she said, and pulled her hands away.

He leaned down and kissed her forehead and murmured, "I know why you are so hungry." He looked into her eyes and growled softly at her. She reached up and feathered his cheek gently with the tip of her fingers. Every time she touched him, it sent a shudder down his back.

"I know I can make you moan louder," she told him, and giggled.

"Yes, I know," he answered her. He offered his hand to her because he knew if they didn't leave this room, they would end up in bed again. She stood and followed him closely, up the stairs to the narrow hall into the dining area. She sat next to him on the white leather chair facing the crystal blue sea.

"Wow! Lots of food," she announced. She looked at the cheeses, more fruit, meats, and all kinds of freshly baked bread. She turned and observed a steward headed her way with eggs. "We can't eat all of this."

"They usually don't cook so much, but Henry must have told them to prepare a hearty breakfast. Help yourself!" Logan told her. They both dug into the food. Logan raised his head from his plate and saw Henry approaching. Henry leaned down on the opposite side of Bailey and whispered to Logan, "This message just came for you. I figured you'd want to know right away." He showed him a piece of paper.

"Thank you, Henry." Henry passed him the note. Logan opened it and immediately lost his appetite. He read the announcement then crumpled the paper tightly in his hand and threw it beside his plate. He sighed heavily.

CHAPTER 6

Bailey kept her eyes on Logan's face. He had no expression; he was just blank. He wasn't eating anymore. He seemed to be distant as he focused his vision toward the endless sea. She touched his arm tenderly. He didn't move an inch. He just sat there, stoic. He seemed to be in his own world. *What was in that message, to change his mood so fast? Why?* She caressed his arm lightly and called his name.

"Logan. Logan, is everything all right?" she asked. He finally glanced her way and gave her a small smile. He wrapped her hand with his and tapped it twice.

"I'm fine. My brother Riker is coming. He'll meet us in St. George," he answered. She sensed there was more to the story by his reaction to the news.

"Oh! I'd love to meet him," she said. As soon as she uttered the words, she was sorry. Logan frowned and turned his face away from her.

"You don't want to meet him. He's not at all what he seems to be. He's arrogant and conceited," he told her. She felt her heart skip a beat in her chest; something was not right. *Why would he not want to see his brother? He must have harmed him badly at some point.*

"I'm sorry," was all she could say. She placed her hands on her lap and waited for him to speak. She wasn't hungry anymore, either.

She noticed a calm slowly settling over Logan's features. He tried to regain his composure. He shifted his weight on his chair. She just sat in silence, waiting. He exhaled a deep breath and turned to her. He took her hands in his, brought them up to his lips, and kissed her knuckles.

"It's not your fault. It's just...he betrayed me. Since then, we don't get along very well. He always thinks he knows what's best for me, and I hate it. He wants to control everything I do, and especially whom I see. A few years ago, he was the primary reason why I didn't get married. He and I are so different from each other. We always end up in some sort of dispute before he returns home," Logan said. He leaned over and kissed her cheek. He reached for his coffee and took a sip. Bailey was speechless. She wasn't sure what to say to him. She felt a lump in her throat that caused her to swallow hard. It seemed his anger had passed, but it was replaced with sadness. He looked away from her to hide his discontent.

"Don't let him bother you. How long is he staying? You can spend your days with me and avoid him. At night we can go to dinner and..." she stopped talking because she still had a cruise to finish with Dakota. *Be realistic! I can't spend all my nights on this yacht. I might not have another night with him. He probably will forget me as soon I re-board the Windstar.*

A sexy grin appeared on his face and his eyes sparkled with joy.

"I have an idea. Why don't you stay with me at night?" he suggested. She couldn't just leave Dakota alone on the ship; or could she?

"I would like nothing more than to be in your arms every night, but I can't leave Dakota by herself. We planned this vacation together, and it wouldn't be right," she answered. She felt a gloominess invade her heart, realizing tonight might be her last night with him. They were scheduled to arrive in St. George in the morning. He was drumming his fingers on the top of the table. His other hand was leaning against his cheek. He was distant again. *What was he thinking about?* Suddenly, he flagged the steward who was passing by to come to the table.

"Could you tell Henry I would like to speak to him, please? Thank you." Logan followed him with his eyes until he disappeared to the other room. He pushed his chair back and stood up. He walked over, wrapped his arms around her shoulders, and bent down to kiss the top of her head.

"You gave me the solution to my dilemma. Finish your breakfast. I'll be right back," he said.

"What solution?" she asked, but he didn't answer her. He stepped away from the table and strolled into the other room. She cupped her mug of coffee and walked to a lounge chair outside, near the bar area. She sat down and enjoyed the rest of her coffee.

After few minutes passed, she looked back in the direction where Logan vanished, but he was nowhere to be seen. She lay back in the chair, wondering where he had gone. She crossed her ankles and closed her eyes, soaking in the heat of the sun and waiting for his return.

Fifteen minutes later, she was finishing her drink when she heard him. Logan waltzed back in the room and sat on the end of her chair. He beamed from ear to ear. He seemed excited about something, but what?

"We are all set! When we arrive in St. George, we can go get Dakota and both of you can sail around the islands with me, on my yacht," he said. Bailey eyes widened in shock and disbelief.

"What are you talking about? I don't know if she'll agree to do that. We already paid for our cruise. You can't make that decision for her," she told him. As much as she would love to do it and spend time with him, she could not make that decision.

"Why not? We'll go meet her tomorrow and explain the situation to her, and bring her back. Listen, I want to spend more time with you before you return home; she will love it. I promise to take you wherever you were supposed to go on your cruise. We'll have a good time and I won't have to deal with my brother so much," he told her.

He laughed as he started to massage her thigh, upward from her knee. She slapped his hand to make him pay attention.

"I would love it, but I'm not sure if you can convince her to come along. It's fine by me," she said, still dumbfounded at his invitation. She liked him and wanted to get to know him better. He had a hold on her, even though they hadn't known each other that long. This was what she longed for; a man who desired her and would do anything just to keep her by his side. She was beginning to be keen on the way he took care of her. *Could he be taking advantage of me? Will he just forget me after my vacation ends?* She didn't want to get her heart broken again.

The rest of the day was spent lying in the sun, absorbing the hot rays while having drinks and stuffing her mouth with the delicious appetizers of chicken kabob, nachos and vegetable dishes prepared by the chef. They were unwinding and lounging around outside in their bathing suits, drinking frozen drinks and watching the sunset on the horizon.

All afternoon Bailey had a reoccurring thought. It kept resurfacing in her mind. She wondered what Logan's brother had done to break up his previously planned marriage. Maybe she should keep her mouth shut, since she hadn't known him that very long. She'd shared his bed, and she wanted to know everything about his life. The past few days had been her happiest times in months.

She was lying next to him on the cushions on the deck, snuggled in his arms. She touched and caressed his abdomen. She rose up on one elbow and looked up at his golden locks, avoiding his blue eyes. She twirled his curls between her fingers, then stopped and glanced away.

"Can I ask you a personal question?" she uttered in a serious tone.

He moved to sit up straighter, still holding his arm around her.

"You can ask me anything," he answered, then stayed quiet and waited for her question. She faced him. She placed her hand on his chest, then lowered her head and rested it on his chest.

"What did your brother do to you that was so bad you don't get along? If it's too private or hurtful, you don't have to tell me. I'll understand," she said. She waited for his explanation. Not a word came out. *It must be really bad.* Finally she couldn't stand the silence between them anymore.

She lifted up and looked into his eyes. "I'm sorry; it's none of my business. You don't have to tell me," she said then pushed up from him. She shouldn't have said anything. His brother must really have pained him. She felt his arms grab her and bring her back against his chest. He held her tight, cocooning her so she could barely move.

"Riker had an affair with my fiancée a few years ago because he didn't want me to marry her. I know it wasn't entirely his fault, but it devastated me. We didn't speak for two years. And now I have you by my side and I don't trust him. I definitely don't want him near you," he said and kissed her forehead. She propped herself up so that her face was inches from his. She kissed him passionately. She shuddered every time her lips touched his. She pulled away just long enough to say, "Well, you don't have to worry, I'm all yours, only yours," then planted her mouth on his. She moved her body parallel to his. She could feel a growing erection against her belly as he massaged her derriere and her upper thigh.

"Let's get out of here before I embarrass myself in front of my crew," he said in a soft voice, groaning. He slapped her butt lightly. He pushed her body away from his. He grinned and said, "You are amazing." He stood and held out his hand out to her. She immediately set her delicate hand in his. He escorted her back to his stateroom for a delightful night of lovemaking.

***

Logan woke up the following morning feeling satisfied. He smiled at the beautiful woman sleeping alongside him. He pushed a strand of hair from her face with his thumb. He closed his eyes to inhale her lavender scent, and enjoyed memories of the previous evening. He was feeling emotions he hadn't felt in years. He understood that he hadn't known her long, but he was content. Happiness or love had not materialized in his life since his brother destroyed all hopes of his trusting another woman.

His mind reflected back to the night he had been working late at the office, reviewing contracts. He called his fiancée, Britney, to let her know he would not be able to meet her for dinner, but she had not answered her phone. He lost track of time when he looked briefly at his watch. It was ten o'clock and he hadn't gotten a hold of Britney. He closed the folder, stood and walked out of the office. There would be time tomorrow to reassess the documents, he remembered thinking, because he longed to be with her.

He used his key to open the door to her apartment, as he had done thousand of times before. Then he heard her laughter coming from her bedroom. Joy had entered his heart with the sound. But as he walked toward her room, he also heard a familiar man's voice. He froze in the hallway at the entrance of her bedroom and eavesdropped. Shock and incredulity invaded him. He didn't want to believe she would betray him, so he turned the knob and pushed open the door. He would never forget the image engraved in his brain when he discovered Britney and Ricker naked in bed. Incredible pain surfaced for years, and ever since that night, he despised his brother.

The following week he bought his yacht, intending to sail around the world. He hadn't been home since the day he left everything behind to try to forget the sorrow they had caused him. Riker had dropped her like a hot potato the next day. The only person Logan asked to join him on his travels was his faithful companion Henry. Riker eventually found him, but all his apologies and excuses were fruitless. He kept coming to visit, even though Logan told him otherwise. Now Logan had a chance at love again with Bailey, and he didn't want his brother anywhere near her.

He was brought back to reality when he felt Bailey's soft hand touch his cheek, followed by the sound of her voice, "Good morning, hot stuff." She looked at him and he wrapped his arms around her and slid her body closer to his. He planted a kiss on her lips and he felt her nipples rub against his skin.

"Good morning to you, too. Did you sleep as good as I did?" he asked as he gave her a silly smirk. He stroked her back. She seemed to be listening for something, as her eyes darted from one side of the room to another.

"What's the matter?" he asked, concerned. Logan frowned with eyebrows together and glanced around the room, wondering what was wrong.

"The boat; it's not moving. I don't feel anything. We must be docked in St. George," she exclaimed as she separated from him. She pushed the sheet away from her body and jumped out of bed. She walked to the window, naked.

"Yes, we're here," she said excitedly, as she pushed the curtain to the side to have a better look of the view. All Logan could see or care about was her exposed buttocks, which he was staring at.

"I really don't mind, but do you do know people can see you through the window? And you are standing there with nothing on, butt naked," he told her. Bailey whipped around, raised her hand to her mouth, and within two steps she was back in the bed beside him, covering herself with the sheet. Logan howled with laughter as he watched her face turn red, mortified.

"Why didn't you tell me they could see me?" she asked. She poked him in the ribs, but he couldn't stop laughing.

He just shook his head at her. "No one can see you, I lied," he said as he continued to chuckle at her. Bailey stuck out her tongue at him and made a grimace. She punched him playfully in the side as he enfolded her in his arms. It took him a minute to regain his composure after teasing her.

"I haven't laughed that much in a long time, my belly muscles hurt," he said, and kissed her.

"Let's get dressed and go find Dakota," she blurted out. She wrestled to free herself from his grip, which didn't take long.

"Are you coming or what?" she yelled. Logan watched her skip toward the bathroom, her hips swaying from side to side, and focused on her round butt. He heard the water of the shower start up; that was his cue. It prompted a hot sexual desire in his veins and he had no more control. He was eager to taste her one more time. He swung himself out of bed and raced to join her in the shower, for a little morning delight before they had to leave to meet with Dakota.

CHAPTER 7

Bailey felt as if she was floating on a cloud. She was having the time of her life with a man she was falling for. Logan was kind, attentive, and she loved every minute with him. She sat outside in the dining area, with her phone in her hand. Logan had gone into town to pick up a few supplies, and he told her he would return within the hour. She dialed Dakota's cell number and waited patiently for her. She looked out toward the pier, watching tourists stroll and spy on the yachts. She could hear Caribbean music and smell the ethnic foods from the restaurants in the background.

"Hey, how are you?" Dakota answered cheerfully.

"I'm just fine. How about you? Sorry I didn't call earlier," Bailey apologized. She picked up her glass of iced coffee to take a sip. She looked up at the clock on the wall. It was only eleven o'clock.

"I'm on vacation. What do I care? So tell me, how's Mr. Logan?" she asked, lightheartedly.

"We're doing great, as a matter of fact. Listen, I need to talk to you about something. A friend of Logan's named Henry is on his way to pick you up at your ship, to escort you back to Logan's boat so we can spend the day together," she explained, hoping Dakota would agree.

"Fancy, fancy!" she joked.

"So who's this guy Henry? What do you want to talk to me about?" Bailey didn't want to tell her the plans over the phone.

"Henry is an older gentleman, tall, grayish hair, he works for Logan. You don't have to be afraid, he's harmless. He should be there within the hour. Could you please go to my cabin and pack me some clothes, like a dress, shorts and a few tops, the essentials? I'll explain when you get here. I can't wait to see you," Bailey told her. Looking out on the dock, Bailey saw a black sedan pulling up near the gangway where they were docked. She watched as a chauffeur got out of the car and opened the back door. A tall man wearing sunglasses, a light-colored hat, and white pants with a white shirt stepped out. She couldn't see his face because the rim of his hat blocked it. *Must be a celebrity or something.*

"Okay, I'll keep a lookout for Henry. See you soon!" Dakota laughed. Bailey heard the sound of a click on the other end of the phone. She glanced at her phone in her hand. She couldn't wait to see Dakota's expression when she saw the yacht. She giggled. She stood up, grabbed her suntan lotion in one hand and her iced coffee in the other. She walked to the lounge chair on the front deck and untied the knot of her cover up, showing off her orange bikini. She wanted to relax and pick up some rays.

Bailey was soaking the sun up when a she had an unpleasant feeling; someone was observing her. She opened her eyes, lifted her head and stared directly at a man standing in front of her. He was Logan's double, only with shorter hair! It was Riker.

"Well, well, who do we have here?" Riker uttered with a smirk on his face. He eyed Bailey from head to toe. Bailey immediately sat up and grabbed her cover up. She wrapped it around herself as fast as she could to cover her body.

"You must be one of Logan's playmates. My name is Riker, I'm his brother," he said, licking his lips. She pursed her lips together and stood up straight. She felt uncomfortable. She held tightly on the sides of her cover up.

"My name is Bailey, and I'm not one of his playmates. I'm a friend," she answered and frowned at him. She pouted sullenly at him. Anger was mounting due to his comment. Her ears were on fire. *How dare he call me one of Logan's toys?*

"A friend, Oh! I'm so sorry. So, where is Logan?" he asked with a sneer. He turned, walked to the bar area, grabbed a bottle of Scotch and a tumbler and poured himself a drink. He raised his glass and asked, "Would you care for one?"

Bailey shook her head. "Logan went in town to pick up a few supplies. He should be back soon. If you'll excuse me." She'd stepped toward the inside of the dining area when she heard him say, "Please, don't leave on my account. Logan will be upset that you didn't keep me company."

Bailey stopped walking, sighed under her breath and turned around to face him. A mischievous smile was on his face. *He is the spitting image of Logan,* she thought, *but their personalities are so definitely opposite. Logan was right. Riker is unscrupulous, but he is Logan's brother.* So, she walked slowly back to the stool at the bar that was furthest from Riker and sat down. She didn't want to be rude.

"I'll have a coke." She watched him pour it and hand it to her.

"Thank you," she said. She avoided looking into his eyes. She took a sip. She didn't want to make conversation with him. *Where was Logan?* She hoped he'd get back soon, because she really didn't want to be alone with Riker. He made her feel uneasy. She shifted and turned her back to him to faced the water.

"So, tell me, how long have you known my brother?" he asked. He walked around the bar and took a seat near her.

"A week or so," she lied softly, without looking in his direction.

"Wow! A whole week! And where did you meet?" he asked. Sneering, he laughed out loud. She watched as he gulped his drink. He walked back to the bar and poured himself another. Bailey decided she'd had enough of his smart comments. She got up from her seat, pushed her drink aside, and turned to walk away. Suddenly, she saw Logan coming her way. *Thank God! I am ready to give this guy a piece of my mind. He might be rich and Logan's brother, but he is ill-mannered. I see why Logan despises him.*

Logan smiled her way and she felt relief as he walked toward her. He slipped his hand onto her back and kissed her on the cheek. Bailey sat back down. Logan put his protective arm on the back of her seat. He maintained an upright position while placing one foot up on the leg of her bar stool.

"Riker, I thought you weren't arriving until later on this afternoon," Logan said. He gave his brother an annoyed look.

"I took an early flight. I couldn't wait to see you, dear brother," Riker replied. He raised his drink and took a mouthful, but kept his eyes on Logan. Bailey could sense the friction between them. She looked at Logan and noticed a tick in his jaw as he clenched his teeth.

"Nice to see you, too. How long do you plan on staying this time?" Logan asked, with a hint of sarcasm. Logan never took his eyes off his brother. Bailey sat quietly, not moving or wanting to get in the middle of what seemed to be an argument waiting to happen, with the scornful comments being tossed back and forth.

"I'm not sure yet. It's depends on when I get bored, I suppose, but right now I'm just going to enjoy the island for a bit," he snickered.

"Fine, enjoy!" Logan jeered. Logan looked at Bailey and touched the small of her back to prompt her to stand. Henry was waiting for them about twenty feet away. She noted that Henry's hands were by his sides, but balled into fists. His eyes, focused on Riker, looked like poisoned darts.

"Let's go find Dakota on the upper deck," Logan softly said to Bailey.

"Sure," she replied without emotion. Logan took her hand in his, looked at Riker with distaste one last time, and led Bailey away from the bar area. Not another word was spoken between the brothers.

***

As Bailey and Logan approached Henry, he relaxed and he smiled at both of them. He loosened the grip of his hands as he nodded to Logan and said, "Miss Dakota is waiting for the two of you upstairs, on the upper deck." He escorted them up the spiral staircase. Bailey saw her leaning against railing, watching the people walking on the pier.

"Dakota!" Bailey said enthusiastically. Dakota whipped around and dashed to her. They embraced each other.

"I was so worried when you didn't show up on the ship night before last. Thank God you sent a message."

"Welcome aboard, let's have a seat and refreshments," Logan said, pointing to the cushioned chairs next to him. They both sat down, next to each other.

"Now, what can Henry get you to drink?" Logan asked.

"I'll have Perrier water, and could you bring us a few bowls of nuts and maybe some cheese, Henry?" Logan asked. Then he sat next to Bailey, extended his legs and crossed his feet.

"We'll have the same, Henry, thank you," Bailey answered for both of them.

"Wow! I was shocked when I first saw this ship. I thought it was a joke. This is a beautiful yacht, Logan," Dakota said, and made eye contact with Bailey. Bailey heard Logan say, "Thank you," A shy smile appeared on his face. *He is so modest. That is one thing I love about him; he isn't like his arrogant bastard brother. Stop it!* She told herself. *You don't know the whole story of what transpired between them.*

"I had the same response, and that was why Logan wanted to bring you here. He has something to ask you," Bailey smiled. Dakota first looked toward Logan, then looked at Bailey. Baily tilted her head toward Dakota. Logan bent forward as he placed his elbows on his knees and touched Bailey's leg. Logan seemed nervous. Maybe he was afraid that Dakota wouldn't agree; when he spoke, his voice was serious.

"Dakota, I was wondering if you would like to join us onboard my yacht, *The Vagabond*, and cruise the islands for the next week or so?" he asked.

Dakota seemed confused. "What!?" She was surprised and worried at the same time. Her eyebrows came together, forming a frown. Not a word was spoken for a moment, until Bailey broke the silence.

"What Logan means is he would like us to give up the cruise on the Windstar, and visit the rest of the islands scheduled on our trip on his boat." Bailey tried to make it clearer.

"Are you pulling my leg?" she finally sputtered, looking at both Logan and Bailey.

They both nodded their heads.

"Then how can I say no? I would love to," she replied excitedly, bouncing in her chair.

***

Logan's heart swelled as he thought of spending more time with Bailey. He sent Henry and a deckhand with Dakota to pick up the rest of their belongings. By late afternoon, Dakota was settled into one of the private staterooms on the ship. The captain was given new orders, and they were all on their way to a new destination. Bailey and Logan were preparing for dinner, after a great day of sightseeing on the island.

Logan lay on top of the covers on his bed, wearing only boxer shorts, with his hands behind his head. He admired Bailey fixing her hair in the mirror. She was dressed in a white cotton dress that accentuated her curves, hugging her hips. She was humming a tune he didn't know but liked, as she brushed her hair. He knew at that instant that he never wanted to be separated from her. This past week had been the happiest he had been in a long time. He had feelings emerge that he hadn't had in years. Even though he had not known her for long, he was falling in love with her. He closed his eyes as he reflected on their fun together and what was yet to come. He was haunted by the idea she might not feel the same way he did. He immediately erased that notion from his mind and reopened his eyes.

"You look beautiful. Why don't you come over here and join me?" he asked her. His eyes were glued to her. She stopped brushing her hair and faced him, leaning her backside against the bathroom counter.

"If you don't get dressed soon, you'll have to explain the reason why you were late for dinner," she teased. She walked forward, bent down, placed her hands on his sides, and kissed him on the lips. He unclasped his hands to surround her body with his arms. She pulled back, tittering by the edge of the bed.

"All right. I'll meet you and Dakota in the dining room, give me ten minutes. Go ahead," he told her. She smiled and blew him a kiss. He pretended to catch it. She grabbed the door handle, opened it, and disappeared behind it.

He'd delayed getting dressed because he dreaded the idea of having to face his brother. Logan wished Riker would just go away, but he knew it wasn't going to happen. So he might as well make the best of a bad situation. He would avoid Riker by being busy with the girls. He rose from the bed and took a few strides towards the closet, resigned to getting dressed.

***

Bailey hurried, walking at a quick pace to go meet with Dakota. She was late, and she hoped Dakota had made herself at home. She turned the corner and crashed straight into a body, accidently stepping on his foot. Bailey stumbled backward, her hands trying to grab onto anything not to fall, but she lost her balance and fell on her butt.

"What the hell is your problem? Watch where you're going, bitch!" It was the voice of a man, in an angry tone. She could smell alcohol in the air. She was mortified, and could feel heat running up to her face.

It was him. Riker looked down at her and started to laugh loudly.. She pushed herself up with her hands and dusted her clothes off.

"I'm so sorry. I didn't see you," she managed to say, but he just raised his eyebrows and kept on chuckling at her. He gazed past her shoulder and gulped down the rest of his drink.

She felt a hand on her right shoulder and turned around to see who was touching her. It was Henry, with a concerned look on his face.

"Are you all right, Miss Bailey?" he asked.

But before she could answer Riker said, "She's just fine, Henry." Riker passed by both of them in the tight hallway and continued along his way. Bailey heard him snicker as he went by both of them. She noticed Henry turned his head slightly and followed him with narrowed eyes, his jaw clenched tight. She put her hand on his arm and said, "I'm okay, Henry. Thank you."

He spun around to glance at her. "He's so..." Henry shook his head and closed his eyes. He sighed heavily.

"Are you sure you're okay, Miss?" he asked again, with a smile.

"Yes. I'm just a little embarrassed, that's all. Thank you again," she said. She scanned the hall to make sure Riker wasn't still in the vicinity.

"Is Dakota in the dining room yet?" she asked.

"Yes, Miss. I was just going to get her another cocktail. May I bring you something to drink?" Henry politely inquired. He touched her arm lightly.

She nodded at him, "I'll have the same, thank you," she answered.

"Very well, Miss, I'll be right back." He turned and walked down the hall, toward the galley. She was not going to let Riker ruin her vacation. She pulled her chin up, put a smile on her face, and headed off to meet her friend.

***

68

Logan had just finished dressing in a beige pair of linen pants and a white shirt. He was applying cologne when he heard a loud knock on his stateroom door. He walked over and opened the door. Standing in front of him was his brother, with a drink in one hand and a folder in the other. He was swaying from one side to the other. Riker leaned his body against the door frame. Logan could tell he was drunk, as he usually was when he stayed onboard. He would say it was his down time, so he would binge drink for days while he was onboard.

Riker would come to visit him a few times a year, mostly when he needed Logan sign business contracts. Their grandmother had a special clause written into her last will. Both boys needed to be equal partners, so Riker couldn't acquire any business deals over twenty million dollars without both signatures on the agreement.

"Hello brother, I brought you contracts that need your signature," Riker said. Logan noticed he was slurring his words. He was definitely inebriated. He extended the folder toward Logan.

"You're drunk! Go sleep it off," Logan told him, in a disgusted tone. Riker burst out laughing. Logan snatched the papers from Riker's hands, turned around and placed them on the side table by the entrance.

"By the way, I bumped into your girlfriend on the way here. I bet she's a nice little piece of ass in bed," he threw at Logan with a snicker. A rush of anger invaded Logan's body. His eyes narrowed, his hands went up and grabbed Riker's shirt collar. Logan pulled him forward until he was inches from his face. He reeked of alcohol. Riker was losing his footing from the alcohol and dropped his glass. Logan stared at him for a moment, and then said, "I'll only say it once. Stay the fuck away from her, or else."

Riker blinked and frowned at his brother. "Or else what?" He clapped his hands over Logan's hands and freed himself from Logan's grip. He took a step backwards and raised his hands to straighten his shirt. Logan took a step forward, his fists tightly clenched.

"Don't worry, little brother, I won't bed her," he said. Riker then moved unsteadily from side to side down the hallway. Riker was twenty feet away when he yelled out to Logan, "Not yet."

Logan heard his roar of laughter echo down the hall. Logan grabbed the handle of the door, stepped back inside and slammed it shut. He stared at the wooden door, trying to calm down. He was trying to control his nerves and breathing. He rubbed his face with his hands and raked his fingers through his locks. *I will kill you if you ever touch her.*

He would not let Riker ruin another relationship. He'd have to warn Bailey to stay away from him, especially when he was drinking. *I cannot leave her alone too long.* He closed his eyes and inhaled deeply, then let it out. He repeated this and massaged his face again. *Calm down, this is what he wants. He wants to put a wedge between you and Bailey. He loves it when I'm miserable, and he's at his best when conflicts arise.* His heartbeat eventually slowed down. Logan opened his eyes, grasped the doorknob, turned it and walked out into the hallway. He scanned the hall, but Riker was nowhere to be seen. He needed to join Bailey and Dakota for dinner, and he would not give Riker the satisfaction of ruining his evening. He quickened his pace and when he saw Bailey, all his worries faded away.

CHAPTER 8

Bailey beamed when she saw her friend Dakota sitting by herself at the table, looking out at the horizon. She had a purple sundress on and was holding a martini.

"Sorry I'm late!" Bailey said. She pulled out a chair and sat next to her friend. The table was already set for dinner, decorated with seashells and tropical flowers. All the dinnerware was sky blue and white.

"Have you been waiting long?" Bailey asked, eyeing her drink. Dakota shook her head.

"What are you having?" Bailey pointed at her glass, and Dakota offered it to her. Bailey picked it up and tasted it.

"Mmm! Pretty good! I think I'll have the same, what is it?" she asked, handing it back to Dakota.

"I'm not sure. It's called a Vagabond. Funny! Henry made it for me. He said it was his specialty, and a secret," she answered. They both laughed. Bailey turned toward the hall as she saw Henry approaching; his eyes admiring the two women. He was smiling at them.

"Good evening, again. Miss Bailey, here's your cocktail," he said, as he put her drink down. He placed a bowl of crackers and an assortment of cheeses on the table, as well.

"Henry, I love these! If it's not too much trouble, tell me, what's in it?" she asked. He shook his head at her in a playful gesture.

"No, as I told Miss. Dakota, it's a secret. But I'm sure you'll enjoy it. I'll be right back," he answered. He turned and walked away to mix more cocktails.

"So what are your plans for tomorrow?" Dakota asked. She sipped her drink, then grabbed a bit of cheese and popped it into her mouth.

"I'm not sure. I might just stay in bed all day," she whispered in Dakota's ear, afraid of being overheard. They giggled like teenage school-girls with a new boyfriend. Dakota elbowed her lightly and laughed.

"What's so funny?" They heard a voice say behind them. They both became silent and twirled around to look at the person speaking. It was Logan. He leaned down and kissed Bailey on the cheek, then sat beside her. He laid his left hand on her knee and waited for an answer, but the girls just started to laugh again. Bailey looked away, not wanting to tell him what she had just told Dakota. She bowed her head, trying to stop the snickering. She finally gained control and grinned at him.

"Okay, now I really want to know..." he teased as he squeezed her knee lightly. She covered his hand with hers.

"We were just trying to figure out what Henry puts in his famous drink called *The Vagabond*," Dakota answered, saving Bailey from embarrassment. She winked at Bailey.

"Yes, what is in it? He won't say." Bailey quickly jumped in as she saw Henry heading for the table with another cocktail in his hand. He placed it in front of Bailey then nodded at her. "Thank you Henry," Bailey said softly and slid it closer.

"It is only rum, Grand Marnier, and cranberry juice with a twist of lemon. What did he tell you? That it's a special drink?" Logan asked. They both nodded.

"Shall I serve dinner soon?" Henry inquired, looking at Logan.

"Yes, that would be perfect, Henry," he answered. He grabbed a handful of crackers and popped a few into his mouth with cheese and said, "Could you please bring me a beer, Henry?" Henry nodded.

"Will Mr. Riker be joining you for dinner?" Henry asked.

Bailey saw that tick in Logan's jaw reappear as he answered, "Hopefully he won't join us. I think he's sleeping it off." Henry took a step back, then turned around and left the room.

"So, what would you girls like to do tomorrow? We could do some sightseeing, or go to the beach, whatever you would like," Logan said. The girls let out a half-suppressed laugh and Dakota looked away.

Bailey turned her head toward Logan, "The beach is fine by me, and maybe some snorkeling. What do you think, Dakota?" she asked.

"Sounds good to me," Dakota replied.

Henry served a dinner to the three of them that consisted of poached salmon with rice, salad, and to finish it off, strawberry cheesecake. They had not seen or heard from Riker.

An hour and a half passed by with the three just relaxing at the table, finishing dinner. They were planning their day between bites. Dakota asked Logan where they might be able to pick up a few more souvenirs on the islands, when a chill ran down Bailey's back. The hair on her neck raised up. She had a feeling someone was watching her. She turned her head to her right, toward the window of the dining room. She saw a person watching them. He was immobile. She couldn't see a face because of the darkness of the night. She was aware of him realizing he'd been seen; then he disappeared behind the wall. *Who was that? Maybe it was one of the crewmembers.* She shook it off and didn't mention it to Logan or Dakota.

"We should go to bed, if we want to have an early start tomorrow and hit the stores before the beach," Dakota mentioned. She pushed her chair back from the table and stood up.

"That's a great idea!" Logan replied. He looked at Bailey with a sexy grin on his face. Bailey extended her hand and slapped his knee gently, rolling her eyes at Dakota.

"Don't listen to him; he has a one-track mind. I'll see you at breakfast," Bailey joked. Dakota nodded. Bailey heard Logan chuckle. As soon as Dakota was out of sight, she felt a hand caressing her thigh.

"We should listen to your friend and go to bed early," Logan whispered, leaning forward to softly bite her ear. She closed her eyes as she inhaled his musky scent. She could feel a wetness spiraling down to her naked shoulder as his lips and tongue kissed her.

A flare of sexual desire rushed between her legs; she yearned to have his nude body on top of hers.

"Yes, I believe we should," she answered. She let her hand slide all the way from his knee to his lower abdomen. He winked at her and stood up.

***

The next morning the girls decided to go do a little shopping for a few hours in town, before they headed out to the beach. They were to meet back at the yacht at noon. Bailey wanted to get a gift for Logan to thank him for his hospitality, and for being such a good host. *Really! Who are you kidding?* she thought, as she walked along the stores in The Esplanade Mall. She wanted to give him something that would remind him of her so he wouldn't forget her, but what? There were only two more stops on their voyage before they would get on a plane to go home.

Bailey sighed as she strolled out of another store empty-handed. *Nothing!*

"I'm never going to find anything. What do you get someone who can buy virtually anything? Any suggestions?" she asked Dakota, slowly walking to the next shop.

"I know exactly what you should get him!" Dakota said in a perky voice. Dakota was pointing, but Bailey couldn't see what Dakota was trying to show her.

"What?" Bailey asked. Dakota grabbed her by the arm and dragged her in front of the window on the opposite side of the walkway. She indicated what she had found.

"Are you kidding?" Bailey asked, staring at a small puppy in the store window.

"Listen, it's perfect. He would love to have a companion when you're gone, and he won't forget that you bought it for him," she reasoned.

Bailey didn't say a word. She stood tapping her index finger on her lips, thinking.

"This is crazy. He's on a yacht! Where is the dog going to go to the bathroom?" she asked Dakota, not taking her eyes off the dog.

"He'll love it. You worry too much. Now come on, let's get it." Dakota signaled her to follow and entered the pet store. Uncertain, Bailey trailed behind her.

Twenty minutes later, Bailey walked out of the pet store with a ten-week-old English bulldog in a cloth travel carrier, strapped over her shoulder. The puppy was white with fawn spots, a pudgy nose, and droopy eyes. The puppy would be Logan's companion when he was lonely, and hopefully it would remind Logan of her.

I hope he loves this dog, otherwise I'm in trouble. What would I do with her? How would I bring her back home? She hurried back to the boat with the young dog in her carrier. She took the last step up the yacht's bridge to meet with Logan. Bailey was excited; her heart started to beat faster, and her palms were sweaty. She lightly wiped her hands on her shorts as she boarded the boat. *What if he doesn't like dogs?* She stopped for a moment to clear her thoughts and figure out what she was going to say to Logan. She held the carrier closer to her hip as she clutched the strap tighter. She continued going forward, up the stairs to the main deck. One step at a time she lifted her feet, which suddenly seemed so heavy. She stopped halfway up to look at the face of the dog that had no name. She was sleeping contently. She loved animals, so what better gift to give Logan?

***

Logan was on the upper deck, looking over the documents that his brother had brought for him to sign. He sat on one of the lounge chairs, with an empty soda can by his side. He was elated that he had not seen or heard from Riker all day. He was distracted from his reading when he saw Bailey and Dakota walking down the pier toward the boat. He watched Bailey's hips sway from side to side as she walked. Her long hair bounced around in the wind. She was carrying a canvas bag on her shoulder. They were laughing and seemed to be having a good time.

He felt a warm sensation of jubilation that she was with him. He smiled to himself. He was glad they were back. He had missed her, even though it only had been a few hours. He wondered what he was going to do when she had to leave in a few days. She brought vivacity back into his life. He had a reason to wake up again, and hope that maybe he would love again. He placed the papers on the side table.

He stood up to go greet them at the gate. She was at the top of the landing when he met her.

"Hey, Sweetheart. I missed you," he said, as he stretched out his arms to hold her tight against him. Then he heard a cry coming from the bag she was holding.

He halted midway. "What was that?" Logan asked glancing at her, intrigued.

"Well, it's a present for you. I wanted to give you something so you wouldn't be alone on this yacht anymore," she quietly said, and unzipped the bag. She reached in and grabbed the bulldog. She placed the little puppy in his arms. His mouth opened with surprise. "Oh my

God, you shouldn't have..." he said, and stroked the top of the puppy's head.

"He's adorable. What's his name?" Logan asked as he lifted up the puppy to see its face.

"It's not a 'him,' it's a 'her.' The pet store owner said they try not to name the animals, so it's up to you," she beamed, a wide smile on her face. He bent down and put the puppy on the deck. They watched as the dog started to sniff and paw her way around the floor. Logan widened his arms then pulled Bailey close to him. He could feel the heat of her body against his. He lowered his head and kissed her on the lips.

"Thank you for thinking of me. I love her already, but what are we going to name her?" he asked. His eyes followed the puppy crawling around on the deck and he held Bailey close to him. No one had ever given him such a thoughtful gift.

"That's going to be up to you, she's yours," Bailey answered. She rubbed Logan's back with one hand.

"I'll name her—Precious. Just like you. What do you think?" he asked. His mouth came down on her lips once more. He wrapped his arms tightly around her, wishing she would never leave his side. They both heard a soft yap that brought them back to reality. They glanced at Precious on the floor, rolling and jumping around with a cloth napkin in her mouth. They both burst out laughing.

***

Riker listened when he heard voices coming from the outside deck area. He spied from the living room as Bailey gave Logan the puppy. He pursed his lips together as a feeling of disgust passed through him. He picked up his martini from the table near him and gulped it straight back. He felt the alcohol slide down his throat, burning. An ugly twisted grimace appeared on his face as he reached for the pitcher and refilled his glass. He didn't like this woman. She wasn't the right kind of woman for his brother, and she was slowly crawling into his brother's heart. *Logan needs an affluent woman, his equal. She's one of those particular women who strive to marry a wealthy man. I will have a background check done on her tomorrow. Logan is getting too fond of her.* Riker made a mental note to call his friend Robert.

He was not going to let her take their fortune from them. He had control of Logan's money right now. He had jurisdiction over the assets of the company. He controlled all the finances, everything really, and he didn't want her messing with it. He intensely eyed the happy couple with revulsion. He guzzled the reminder of his drink and felt it burn again as it went down. He tossed his glass down on the table. He wiped his mouth with the back of his hand and with long strides headed toward the twosome. When he arrived at the entryway of the open deck, Riker leaned his shoulder against the frame, crossing his arms upon his chest.

"Where did you get the mutt?" he asked in a condescending tone as he glanced down at the dog. Logan looked up at him immediately and said, "She's not a mutt. She's a bulldog." Riker chuckled to himself. Logan bent down, picked up the puppy and held her close to his chest. He stroked her.

"So sorry, my mistake," Riker apologized sarcastically.

"Did you finish reviewing the acquisitions I gave you?" Riker inquired. He stepped forward to stand in front of his brother, and totally ignored Bailey by his side.

"I'm halfway through it. I only have to study some more numbers, then I'll give you my decision," Logan told him. He wrapped his free arm around Bailey's waist and pulled her closer to him. Riker disliked the look he gave her. It was the same one he had given another woman a few years back, the one he'd wanted to marry. Riker had made sure that it didn't happen. He would have to fix this situation as soon as possible.

"I need it done by tomorrow, understood?" he ordered Logan in a harsh tone. He'd turned around and started to lurch away, when he stopped for a moment. He slowly swung around on his heels and pointed at Bailey.

"Keep your hands off her, and maybe you might finish on time!" he ordered, still pointing at Bailey. Logan's eyes darted toward him.

"I'll keep that in mind, but I'll do as I please," Logan replied. Riker noticed a sudden jerking movement in his jaw. He knew Logan was furious at him for the comment, but he didn't care about his brother's feelings. He needed the reports. They were more important to him than Logan spending time with his 'missy.' Riker reversed his position. Holding his head high, he walked away like the ruthless CEO he had grown to be, over the years.

Riker retreated to his stateroom. He sat down on the far side of his bed. He reached into his pocket and took out his cell phone. He scrolled down through addresses and numbers until he came to the name of Blake Black. Black was a private investigator he often used when he wanted to collect information on a certain individual. He waited patiently with the phone glued to his ear. Two rings later he heard a familiar voice.

"Blake Black Detective Agency, how may I help you?" the person on the line answered.

"Blake, this is Riker St. James. I need your services. Could you get a background check on a person named Bailey Winters? She's in her mid-thirties, and she lives in a town named Newton, outside the Boston area." Riker didn't know much about her, but one thing he knew for sure was she wasn't right for her brother.

"Okay, what else do you have on her?" Blake asked.

"I think she mentioned she worked in veterinary clinic as a secretary. That's it. You can reach me at this number," Riker said, looking outside his window at the pier area.

"Very good. I'll get back to you when I get information," Blake said. Riker clicked the off button and the phone was dead. He placed his cellphone back into his pocket. *I will get rid of her if it's the last thing I do. I won't let you drag my brother down. Maybe I should have a face-to-face talk with her when Logan isn't around. Yes, that's what I'll do.*

CHAPTER 9

The last morning arrived too fast for the girls. They would be leaving for the airport in the evening to catch their flights home. They were back in Barbados, where their journey had first started. It had seemed so far away as she thought of how much she liked a man she had just met ten days ago. But she knew how she felt. Deep down, she didn't want to be separated from him. She didn't know where she stood with him, but she hoped he felt the same. Bailey's eyes were closed while sunbathing alone on the top deck. She was feeling a little sad. It was their last day, but she was optimistic their relationship would continue to blossom, even though they were apart. They would find a way to be together. She was hopeful.

She had been outside for an hour, waiting for Logan to finish reading his business papers.

"I'm so sorry, Bailey, but the faster I finish with these contracts the quicker Riker will leave and we will have time to be alone. I shouldn't be more than a few hours," he assured her during breakfast.

"I understand. Don't worry about me. I'm happy just lying in the sun. I'll be fine," she said, and hugged him. She really wanted to spend every minute of the last day with him. He kissed her cheek, then departed to his office to finish his work. She sat on one of the lounge chairs, absorbing the warm rays of the sun, while reading People's magazine. Dakota went to the flea market that was being held near the pier for last minute gifts.

Bailey was reading an article when she sensed someone watching her. She lifted her head from her magazine and spotted Riker nearing her. He had a cocktail in hand, as usual, and his glassy eyes appeared to see through her. She didn't want to be alone with him. She swung her legs to the side of the chair, grabbed her cover-up and pulled it on. She was about to stand and leave when he spoke, "Don't leave on my account. Sit. I want to speak to you anyway." He sat down in the chair next to her.

"What would you need to talk to me about? We have nothing in common," she answered him and stood up. She was kind of trapped between the two close chairs, since he'd laid down. She would have to jump over his legs to get away from him.

"Ahh! But we do have Logan in common. Please, sit," he ordered her, in a dry tone. Bailey was taken aback by the harsh sound of his voice. Without a word, she slowly bent down and sat again, on the edge her chair. She held the magazine tightly as she laid her hands on her knees. Her body was shaking slightly, and her heart beating faster than usual. She felt stressed being alone with Logan's brother, wondering what he wanted to say to her. She knew how scornful he had been toward her since they had met. They were so close, their knees were almost touching.

She glanced up at him and tried to put up a front. She waited for him to speak.

"So tell me, what are your plans concerning Logan after you leave this yacht?" he asked her, keeping his eyes on her. She couldn't move and didn't know what to say.

"I...I don't know. We haven't talked about it," Bailey answered him quietly. He lifted his cocktail and gulped down the rest of his drink.

"I have been watching you cling to him like he was yours. Well, he isn't yours. Maybe you should move on. You should leave this boat and not look back. You are not our kind of woman. He shouldn't be spending any more time with you. Well, for sex maybe. You're just another playmate, like all the other ones before you. He loves them and leaves them. You have no future together. He needs a strong, powerful woman, not a woman who's out to acquire his wealth and works as a secretary," he snarled the words at her.

Bailey was outraged by what he had just told her. She swallowed hard. She stood up quickly, almost losing her balance because of trying to leap over him. She wanted to slap him. She wanted to yell at him, but she kept her cool.

"How dare you say such a thing! First, I don't care about his money, and I am not his playmate," Bailey said, with gritted teeth. She was about to walk away when she heard him say, "Are you sure about that? Keep away from him."

Bailey ran as fast as she could back toward her stateroom. Tears stung her eyes as she hurried down the hall. A tear fell down her cheek. She put her hand over mouth to suppress a cry. *I am not just his playmate! I can't believe that.* She wasn't paying attention where she was going and suddenly she was face to face with Henry in the hallway. He frowned, with his eyebrows drawn together in concern when he saw the tears swimming in her eyes. He reached out to touch her arm and looked her in the eye.

"Miss Bailey, are you okay? What's the matter?"

"I'm fine Henry, thank you," she whispered, but a sob escaped. She ran to her cabin.

***

Logan sat behind his desk, pouring over the documents Riker had brought when he heard a knock on the door. He laid his papers down on the desk and turned his attention to the interruption. He looked up to see Henry marching into the office. He came right up to his desk. *Strange, Henry is usually a calm man. Something is not right.* Henry was obviously agitated. He was breathing hard and he kept closing and opening his fists.

"What's wrong, Henry?" he asked. Logan could tell he was trying to compose himself before he spoke. Henry stood erect in front of him, shut his eyes for just an instant and said, "I just met Miss Bailey in the hall, and she had tears in her eyes. She's crying. I thought you should know."

"What did she say? Where is she?" Logan asked. He pushed his chair backward and stood up. Precious looked up at him, then jumped around on the floor.

"She didn't say anything," he replied. Logan sprinted around the desk and toward the door. As he made his way past Henry, he continued, "I think she was going to the stateroom. I hope she's all right, sir." Logan didn't stop to answer as he dashed up the stairs, jumping them two at a time. *Who or what had hurt her? What had happened to make her cry? Was she hurt?* His concern mounted with every step he took. His mind was in a frenzy with questions. He pushed ahead until he was in front of their bedroom.

He grabbed the doorknob, swung the door open, and entered. There she was by the dresser, emptying the drawers and putting her clothes into her suitcase. Her eyes were red and her face was wet. He could tell she was upset, but why? She glanced at him, but moved her head away from him. He approached her cautiously until he was standing next to her. She didn't utter a word and continued to pack her things.

"Bailey, are you okay? Why are you packing? What happened? Why are you sad?" He bombarded her with questions. She wouldn't look at him, or answer him. He reached out and touched her arm lightly. She pulled away from his affection and stopped for a slight moment.

Her sight was still on her suitcase. He watched as she walked to the bathroom to retrieve her cosmetics and hair products. She placed them neatly inside the bag and zippered the pocket, never laying her eyes on him.

"Please stop, Bailey! Talk to me," he pleaded in a soft tone.

"What's the matter? Did I do something to hurt you?" he asked, wanting to communicate with her. Logan took another step to her and extended his hand to stop her again.

"Don't touch me! I'm leaving," she wheeled away from him. Logan felt pain in his heart, as if someone had stabbed him. His mouth dropped open. He ran his fingers through his hair. He was confused.

"Bailey, I don't want you to leave. I love you! Please talk to me," he pleaded. He watched her, and she finally stopped packing. He noticed a small tremor in her hands.

"You love me? Ha! Just like all the other playmates you bring on your yacht, I suppose. I'm going home as scheduled, this afternoon. Thanks for the good time," she hurled his way. Shock invaded him instantly.

"What are you talking about? I don't think that of you at all. Don't leave, I don't want you to go," he managed to say. He stood in shock. He did not understand. *What had brought this on? Fight for her, don't let her leave, you love her!* He was frozen with sadness and shock. He was unable to unscramble what she was telling him. This was a nightmare that he couldn't wake up from. She started packing again, then zipped up her small suitcase and pulled it off the bed. She rolled past him, case in hand, without another word or a glimpse his way. She departed in silence.

***

Bailey couldn't get off the yacht fast enough. On her way off *The Vagabond* she asked one of the deckhands to tell Dakota she would meet her at the airport, and stepped upon the dock as quickly as possible. She heard her name being called out from behind her, but she didn't hesitate. She kept her stride. She was afraid if Logan came after her, or said anything else to her, she wouldn't be able to hold her heartache. She would crumble to pieces in front of him. She didn't want his pity; most of all she didn't want him to see that she did love him. Even in the short amount of time they had known each other, she knew she loved him. She never looked back. Tears stinging her eyes, she distanced herself from him. *It was for the best.* She could no longer hold back her sorrow. She let the tears flow down her cheeks.

Bailey didn't stop walking until she was out of sight and far away from the yacht. Several passersby gawked her way, but she ignored them and kept moving forward. Her legs were weak and still shaking from the confrontations she'd endured—first with Riker, then Logan. She dragged her suitcase behind her until her arms ached.

She saw a bench near a park and slumped on the seat. Her hands came up to her face, covering her uncontrollable sobs as she sat unable to move. Wretchedness invaded her soul. Her mind was blank except for one sentence of Riker's that kept resonating. "You're just another playmate, like all the other ones he's had before you."

After about fifteen minutes, she had no more tears. The well was dry. She reached into her pocketbook for a Kleenex. Bailey mopped her tears from her cheeks. She brushed her hair from her face with her fingers and lifted her head up. She planted her feet and with all the strength she had left in her body, rose up. She took a few steps toward the street, raised her arm and flagged a taxi. Extending her hand, Bailey gripped the handle and opened the back door. She pushed her suitcase in, slipped inside, and sat down.

"Where to, Miss?" The cabbie asked.

"Grantley Adams International Airport, please," she told him. She laid her hands in her lap and turned her face toward the window.

She blindly observed the scenery of the town passing her by, and tears started to fall down her cheeks again.

***

Logan stretched out on the bed, leaning against a pile of cushions, in his stateroom. Precious was sleeping by his side. He kept petting her head gently. He had not moved from this spot since Bailey left, eight hours ago. It was now nighttime. Tears had appeared in his eyes when he watched her walk up the pier with her bag in tow. *What had gone so wrong? What had he done to make her leave so abruptly?* His heart was broken. For once in his life, he had found a woman who made him happy. She hadn't cared if he had money or not. She was uncomplicated and genuine. *I even told her I love her, but for some reason she didn't believe me. Why?*

He glanced down at the puppy beside him. What a perfect gift! No one had ever given him such an ideal present. Precious was special. Bailey knew he was a loner and needed someone near him. Logan lifted his head when he heard a light knock on his cabin door.

"Come in," he said. He did not move from his spot. The door opened and Henry appeared, with soup and a sandwich on a tray. He closed the door behind him.

"Logan, I brought you something to eat, sir." Henry set the tray next to him, on the bedside table. Logan wasn't hungry.

"Henry, do you know if someone on board said something to Bailey to make her leave?" Logan asked.

"Logan, if I may?" Henry said, standing at the foot of his bed. He was a servant, yet Logan always treasured his advice. Logan took his eyes off of Precious to glance up at Henry and nodded.

"Logan, if you want this girl in your life, go after her. She is sweet and I think she's a good fit for you. I have never seen you as joyous as you've been these past ten days," he said, and waited for a response.

Logan didn't say a word. Henry added, "As for your question, the only person on this yacht that would have the nerve to say anything to her would be Riker. I discreetly asked the staff if they knew something. One of the deckhands said he saw Riker talking to her just before she departed today."

Logan felt a wave of anger. It invaded his whole body. He sighed heavily.

"Did he overhear what the conversation was about?" Logan got up and started pacing.

"No sir," Henry answered. He turned and exited the room. Logan heard the door close. *Riker probably sent her away. Who else would have the balls to say anything? What lies did he tell her? It must be pretty bad. I should have known better and pieced it together before now.* "Bastard!" he said under his breath.

He swung the door open, Precious wobbling behind him on his heels. Logan marched up the staircase to find his brother. He could barely breathe. Rage consumed his mind and his body so much he trembled. He clenched his hands. *Concentrate, don't be a fool.* He stopped abruptly by the outside doorway when he saw his brother on the main deck. *Calm down! If you want information, you need to be relaxed to talk to him. Otherwise you'll just get into another argument, and you won't get anywhere.* He shook his hands loose and rolled his shoulders back. He closed his eyes for a moment, then stepped into the fresh air. He wanted to know what had been said between Bailey and Riker.

Logan strolled to the bar area with Precious trotting behind him. He reached into the bar fridge and pulled out a beer, a Corona. He twisted off the cap as he slowly moved toward Riker, who was sitting on one of the loungers. There was a warm breeze off the ocean, and the stars were out. Logan wished Bailey was still here and in his arms, so he could cuddle with her as they had done so many nights. *Focus!* He spread out on one of the chairs next to Riker, scooped up the puppy, placed her on his knees, and crossed his ankles.

"Hey, Brother, how's it going?" Riker mumbled. As usual, he'd had too much to drink and was drunk. Riker was holding another straight-up Grey Goose, in a glass with ice. He raised his glass to Logan.

"I'm good," Logan answered casually, and clinked his beer bottle against Riker's glass. He took a sip, trying to keep his fury in check. He felt the beer cool down his throat as he wondered how he was going to breach the subject of Bailey. He petted the dog's back, waiting for Riker to start the conversation about Bailey.

"So, did you finish with the documents yet?" Riker asked. He looked straight ahead at the lights of the town as he gulped down his vodka.

"Not yet. I'll have more time now that Bailey has departed," Logan said, in a steady voice with no emotions. He knew his brother. In time, Riker would run his mouth and tell him everything he needed to know. Logan sat up, scooting to one side of his chair to face his brother. He picked up his puppy under her belly and placed Precious next to him on the cushion.

"So you're finished with another playmate. This one was definitely not at your level at all. Hell for a roll in the hay, well that's different and I told her so," Riker said and glanced at his glass. Logan felt his temper mounting, but he was trying to remain calm. He swallowed hard and kept quiet for another minute.

"Oh! I need another one," Riker said. He stood up and almost tripped on his own feet. He basically stepped backward, reach out his hand for balance and caught the back of a lounger just in time for support. He burst out laughing at the mishap, but continued slowly to the bar. He leaned against the bar counter with his entire bodyweight, picked up the bottle of vodka, and poured the vodka straight into his mouth.

"What do you mean she wasn't my level? Because of our money?" Logan asked casually. He rose and walked over to stand next to Riker, with his beer in his hand.

"Exactly. She's a fucking secretary, for God's sake! What else, but her body would you..." He didn't have a chance to finish. Logan set down his beer and grabbed his brother's shirt collar with both fists. His face was a few inches from Riker's mouth. Logan could smell his alcoholic breath. Logan slightly turned his face as he gritted his teeth and frowned at his brother.

"What else did you say to her? Did you tell her to leave?"

Riker closed one hand over his brother's wrist as he chuckled.

"I told her you love 'em and leave 'em, and she needed to move on," Riker answered between snickers. Logan jerked him against the counter with all his might, still holding onto his shirt.

"You fucking asshole! How dare you speak to her that way! You are to leave this yacht immediately, or God help me, I'll..." Logan screamed at him with revulsion, but was so angry he couldn't finish his threat. His rage was still building. *How could he send her away? He was the reason she left. She is the love of my life, and now she's gone because of what Riker told her.* He was not going to let Riker ruin this for him again.

"Oh, get real! You're overreacting. She's just a tramp, and a gold digger," Riker blurted out. He couldn't say another word before Logan shoved him toward the deck floor. His tumbler went flying through the air and shattered on the deck. Riker lost his balance, arms flailing wide as he fell hard on his butt, then flat on ground.

"Get the fuck off my boat! Leave now! Leave, now, before I...," Logan yelled loudly, with his fists balled up, ready to hit Riker. His eyes were like fiery darts.

"Logan, you can't be serious. She's just a slut. Can't you see that?" Riker said, pushing himself up on his elbows.

Riker looked up at Logan with a vacant expression, but before he could plead his case with his brother, he heard Logan howl, "Henry!" Henry approached with great haste.

"Yes, sir," Henry answered. He glanced at Riker, who was on the floor, now on his knees trying to get up by leaning against the lounger.

"Henry, escort my brother off my boat immediately, before I do something I'll regret," Logan instructed. Logan took two steps to his chair, where the puppy was playing, and picked up Precious in his arms. He stopped again in front of Henry and said, "Also, could you tell the captain to set course for Boston as soon as possible? I'm going to get Bailey back."

Henry grinned happily at him, nodding. "Right away, sir," Logan marched past both of them, never looking back even when Riker called his name. He just kept walking toward his cabin, with Precious cuddled in his arms.

CHAPTER 10

Two days passed and Riker was still beside himself, outraged that his younger brother had thrown him off his yacht—and over someone like Bailey! *She only wants his fortune, she doesn't care about him.* The more he thought of her, the more he despised the woman. He sighed heavily. He stood on the balcony of his newly-found hotel room, at the Sandy Lane Hotel in Barbados. His head was pounding; he raised his hands and rubbed his temples. It was probably from all the drinking, or maybe the stress his brother was inflicting on him because of this girl. Fresh air blew against his face, but this beating pain was constant. His hands gripped the railing of the terrace tightly as he overlooked the people strolling in the gardens below. His eyes darted to his right where his Grey Goose cocktail, untouched, sat on the plastic table.

Riker pursed his lips and closed his eyes as his mind wandered back to his brother. *How dare he treat me that way, after everything I've done for him? Especially over a selfish girl who dazzled him in the bedroom. Any woman could do that. She was only using him for his money! Over the years I've let him do as he pleased, gallivanting around the waters of the world, while I work my ass off to expand and double our empire. Logan wouldn't have what he has without me. Ungrateful!*

He reached into his pocket and took out his phone. He dialed Blake's number to find out what other information he'd found about this tramp. He sat down in the chair on the balcony. He drummed his fingers on the table while he waited for Blake to answer.

"Hello, Black investigations," he heard Blake say.

"Blake, it's Riker St. James. What did you find for me?" he asked, massaging his left temple with his fingers.

"Well, she doesn't have any criminal records. She works as a secretary in Newton, a town on the outskirts of Boston, at a Veterinary Clinic on Main Street. She's worked there for the past ten years. She lives alone, in a small bungalow at sixty-eight Garden Street in the same town. She has about ten thousand dollars saved up, in a TD bank account. She doesn't have any major credit card debts. You can learn a lot by examining someone's garbage," Blake chuckled a bit. Riker walked through the open patio doors to go back inside his suite. He sat down in the chair at the desk. He pulled a piece of paper and a pen out from the drawer. He wrote down the addresses of her work and residence.

"I'll call you if I need anything else," Riker pushed the off button of his phone, cutting Blake off. He took his Black Centurion American Express credit card out of his wallet, turned it over, and dialed the concierge's number on the back of the card. He told the concierge to book him a suite at the Four Seasons Hotel in Boston. He then dialed his pilot's private number, telling him to get his plane ready to travel to Boston. Riker would leave as soon as it was ready to fly.

***

It had been a week since Bailey left Logan in the Caribbean. She sat at her desk at the vet's office, brooding about Logan. She couldn't concentrate. She kept staring at her paperwork; everything was slow to register in her attention. She shuffled papers from one pile to another, and had to start over because of some idiotic error. Her mind kept wandering back to Logan. She reminisced about the time she spent with him on the yacht, and the last conversation they had before she stormed off the yacht. The biggest mistake she had made was quitting; maybe she should have listened to what Logan had to say instead of cutting him off so briskly.

She shouldn't have listened to Riker. She should have told him off. She wasn't prepared for what he had called her. She should have been more understanding about the situation. Bailey was sorry now that she had been so quick to blame Logan. She should have given him a chance to explain, and not paid attention to the hurtful words Riker had said about her. The most unexpected thing she'd learned was when Logan told her he loved her. *He said he loves me! How could I have been so stupid, and leave him so easily?* She knew deep down that she felt the same way. She was too preoccupied, believing the accusations from Riker instead of trusting in Logan.

She went back to work the day after she arrived home, to try to get things back to normal and forget Logan. She hadn't succeeded. He was the only thing on her mind. When her coworkers asked about her cruise, all she could say was that she had a fabulous time. She would not elaborate because it hurt too much. She avoided questions by pretending she needed to catch up on her duties. Days went by in a blur of doing her tasks. Patient after patient would bring their animals in for treatment, and she would greet them, but her mind was always on Logan.

Nights were the worst because she was alone. Her tears would cloud her vision at the thought of what could have been if she had given him a chance. Dakota tried talking to her, but she clammed up. Bailey was unable to talk about what had happened on the yacht. It just hurt too much.

A few days later, after lunch, she was in the back room filing medical documents when she was interrupted by one of the vet's assistants, Theresa.

"Bailey, there's a man in the reception who would like to talk to you. You better go see him. He is so fine," she said, taking half the files from Bailey.

"Who is it, old man Robert?" Bailey laughed and placed the folders in the cabinet. This lonely, retired gentleman in his late seventies always wanted to chat with her when he brought in his dog.

"What does he want?" Bailey asked. She glanced Theresa's way and stopped filing for a second.

Theresa shook her head and shrugged. "It's not him. The guy wouldn't give his name. He wants to talk to you," Theresa informed her.

Bailey raised her eyebrows and handed Theresa the rest of the files. She walked down the small corridor to the front of the office, toward the waiting area. She arrived at the entrance and quickly scanned the room. There was only one person in the room. Her legs went weak and began to tremble. Her hand automatically covered her mouth in surprise when she realized who was standing in front of the window. He had his back to her, but she would know his stance anywhere. Her heart filled with joy when she saw him. He was dressed in a blue suit.

"Logan," she whispered as her eyes locked on him. She watched as he slowly turned around to face her.

"Hi, Bailey," he said and stepped toward her. He stared down at her. He stood two feet away from her. She didn't know what to say; she was without words. A feeling of dread invaded her. Her surprise turned to hatred when she realized it was Riker, not Logan. *Why was he here? What did he want?* She had to brace herself against the door frame. Her hands immediately formed fists.

"What are you doing here?" she questioned him in a low voice, not taking her eyes off him and still unable to move.

"I came to see you. Is there a place where we could talk in private?" Riker asked in a calm, business like tone, never taking his eyes off her.

"I have nothing to say to you. Now, would you please leave?" she answered, and turned to go back to work.

As she turned, she heard him say, "It concerns Logan."

She stopped in mid-stride, immediately. She paused and closed her eyes for a moment. Just hearing Logan's name made her heart skip a beat, and brought tears to her eyes. She composed herself, took a deep breath, and blinked the tears away from her eyes. She pivoted on her heel to face Riker.

"What about him? Is he okay?" she asked. Riker stood facing her with a conceited, smug smile.

"He's fine. We need to talk, it's about Logan," he repeated. *What could they have to talk about?* She watched Riker reach into his inside pocket of his jacket and take out a business card, with an address written on the back. He handed it to her. She took the card without a word.

"Meet me here at five o'clock today, we'll talk then," he said. Four long strides and he was at the front door. He turned back toward her and added, "Don't make me come looking for you." Out the door he went.

She had nothing to say to this man, so why would she want to go? But it was related to Logan, so how could she not meet him? She detested how Riker treated her. She had no respect for him. Her stomach turned sour every time she was near him. What could he want to discuss with her? The only thing they had in common would be Logan, and he wasn't in the picture anymore.

Stunned at his words, Bailey couldn't move. She could feel her legs were about to give way, so she sat down on the nearest chair, right next to her. She looked at the card. It was Riker's business card. She turned it over to look at the address written on the back. *What the hell does he want from me?* The only reason she could think of would be because it pertained to Logan. It piqued her interest, but other than that she didn't feel she had anything to discuss with Riker.

The rest of the afternoon Bailey kept an eye on the clock as the minutes ticked away. She wasn't herself. Her coworkers asked her if she was all right. She wouldn't answer them, all the while trying to keep upbeat. Her mind was not on her work, so around four o'clock she told her boss she didn't feel well and left work early. She had not been herself after the encounter with Riker.

***

Logan was stretched out on a chair on the rear deck, gazing out the endless blue water of the ocean. He could feel the sway of the boat as the ship crawled like an iceberg toward Boston. He wanted it to go faster, but the captain told him he was doing his best. He was tired, unable to sleep at night or eat much. He felt empty inside now that Bailey was not by his side. He missed her laughter, her touch, and most of all, her unpretentious ways. He could still smell her perfume on the pillowcase, and when his hand swept the empty space on the bed where she slept, it crushed him. He had to win her back.

Precious made him smile, and she amused herself with a ball near him. It had been three days since they had left Barbados, and he yearned to see her again. His mind replayed the last conversation with Bailey a thousand times. Now he could see the anguish she'd tried to hide from him, due to Riker's words. She didn't want to tell him what had transpired for fear of wounding him. If only she had said something, but he knew she was too humble to mention anything; afraid it might cause him pain.

The captain told him they would arrive in Boston by late afternoon. He looked at his watch and sighed. It would be three more hours before they would dock. The minute the ship anchored, he was going to go find her. He closed his eyes, hoping to rest his mind from the events that had come to light with Bailey, and especially with Riker, in the last few days.

Over the years he had not spoken to or faced Riker for his indiscretions. He refused to subject himself to Riker's wrath or his dirty schemes any longer. He was determined to get Bailey back. He didn't care about his brother ideas and opinions. It was his life, and his decisions to make. He would live it how he pleased and with whom he loved. His eyelids felt heavier. He finally closed them as he rolled on his side. He gave away to sleep, hoping when he woke up they would be in Boston.

***

Bailey parked across the street of the Joe's American Bar and Grill restaurant on Newbury Street, where she was supposed to meet Riker. She sat behind the steering wheel of her red Honda for half an hour, debating if she should go in or not. *Logan might need her, but why would Riker approach her?* It was a public place so she shouldn't be afraid, but she was. She had butterflies in her belly just thinking about Riker. She knew all he wanted was to alienate her from Logan. She loved Logan, and that alone was reason to take a chance.

She picked up her pocketbook from the passenger seat and swung it over her shoulder. She opened the car door and stepped out. The cool wind assaulted her as she crossed the street, and she quickened her pace. Within two minutes, she was standing in the front entrance. She looked around at the mahogany tables lining the large windows, overlooking Newbury Street. The patrons glanced outside at the people passing by on the street. She couldn't spot Riker. A young lady with long brown hair, dressed in a black outfit holding menus, approached her.

"Good evening, can I help you?" she asked politely.

"I'm meeting Mr. St. James. He's a tall blond man, in his thirties. Has he arrived yet?" she asked.

"Yes, he has. Follow me, please," she replied. She walked down the few stairs to the area on her right, where numerous leather booths and a full bar were located. Bailey followed close behind her until she arrived at the last booth down the aisle.

"There you go. Your waiter will be with you momentarily," she told Bailey, then turned and walked away. Bailey slowly slid into the seat. She looked at Riker across the table, his hand on a martini glass as usual.

"Nice of you to come. Would you care for a drink?" Riker asked her, taking a swallow of his drink. Bailey was too nervous to answer, so she just shook her head. She sifted her weight in the seat and found some inner strength.

"No, thank you. Why did you want me to meet you? Is Logan okay?" she asked, in a strong tone. She was determined to get to the bottom of this encounter as soon as possible. She didn't want to stay near him any longer than she had to. Just sitting near Riker made her stomach turn upside down. The worst of it was that he looked identical to her love. Just sitting across from him reminded her so much of Logan. It broke her heart she couldn't be with Logan. She missed him so much. The two men were so similar in appearance that it was eerie. A chill ran down her back.

"Well, I came to make you a proposal." He gulped the rest of his martini and examined the menu. He continued, "I hear they have delicious burgers." His eyes remained on the menu.

"I lost my appetite when I sat down. What kind of deal? I have nothing you would want," she told him. She was at the end of her patience with this man. The waitress was suddenly standing at their booth, ready to take their order. Bailey was not at all hungry.

"What can I get you? Have you decided?" she asked courteously, while holding her notepad.

"I'll have the American burger and another martini, what about you Bailey?" Riker said, and grinned at her.

She looked at the waitress and said, "Just water, please."

"Okay, I'll be right back," she answered and picked up the menus.

"What do you want from me? You said it concerned Logan," she asked again and sighed heavily. He smiled broadly at her. She wanted to get up and leave, not stay to listen to him and his arrogance. She really needed to know why he had come to see her. One of her legs had a nervous tremor so badly it bounced up and down underneath the table. She watched him reach into his jacket pocket and pull out a white envelope. He placed his hand over it on the table, and slowly slid it toward her. He kept his hand on it and his eyes on Bailey.

"This is the proposal. In this envelope is a cashier's check for one hundred thousand dollars in your name. It is yours, to do with as you please. The only condition is that you never see my brother Logan, ever again," he told her, never taking his eyes off her.

Bailey felt as if an elephant was sitting on her chest. She could not breathe. She felt her blood drain from her face. Her mouth opened, but no words came out. He pulled his hand away, leaving the envelope near her. She directed her eyes on the envelope and then glanced up at him. She was literally speechless, and her mind whirled in disbelief. *He must know something that I don't, because why would he make such an offer to me? Was Logan going to reappear in my life?*

"Why?" was the only word that she could utter. She sat still, not moving a muscle.

"Do we have a deal? One hundred thousand dollars just to stay away from him. Think about it. You want to open a shelter for animals. This would be a nice start," he said.

She loved Logan more than any amount of money and if he came back to her, she would embrace him with open arms. "Answer my question," she insisted. "Why?"

Not a word came out of his mouth. He titled his head and gave her a wicked smirk that made her want to vomit. He chuckled under his breath at her. She quickly pushed the envelope away as if it were burning her. Her trembling hands tightly clutched her pocketbook. Bailey slid out of her seat, stood up, and said, "No, thank you."

She walked away, but stopped when she heard Riker say, "Don't be a fool, take the money. You are all wrong for him."

She never turned around. She started walking again, moving toward the front door without acknowledging him. She ran blindly to her car, her hands trembling as she opened the driver's door. She quickly sat down and rested her head on the steering wheel. She tightly gripped the bottom of the wheel. She tried to regulate her breathing, taking long breaths. Bailey closed her eyes and reassessed what had just taken place in the restaurant. *Why would he offer me money, unless he knows that Logan is coming back to me?* She knew Riker disliked her being with his brother, but she never imaged he would go to the length of offering her money to stay away from him. She truly loved Logan. She knew in her heart he felt the same for her. She smiled and burst into loud, happy laughter. *Logan is coming to Boston!*

***

Riker sat in the booth, watching Bailey walk away from the restaurant. He snatched the envelope from the table and placed it back in his suit pocket. He felt a bit disappointed, and surprised, she hadn't jumped at the opportunity for extra cash. Now he would have to take other means to get her away from Logan. He could not let his brother take up with that kind of woman. She was not what the family expected, or up their standards for him. *What could she bring to the table? Nothing worth talking about; she had no money, no prestige and no education. She definitely is not for him. Logan needs to find himself another woman that fits in his class bracket, but first I have to mend the rift between Logan and me.*

The waitress appeared with his food and martini. She set it in front of him and told him to enjoy his meal. He took a gulp of his drink. He wondered what he was going to say to Logan to rectify his situation. He lost his appetite at the thought, and looked at his plate in disgust.

He pushed his plate away. He reached into his pocket, took out his wallet and threw a fifty-dollar bill on the table. He grabbed his martini and guzzled it down. He had a lot of conniving to do if his plan to break them up was to work. First, he had to find out when Logan would arrive in town, so he could start mending their relationship. He slid out of the booth and casually walked out of the restaurant. He stood by the entrance of the bistro and hailed a cab that was passing by. He told the driver to take him back to the Four Seasons Hotel. He had a few phone calls to make, and didn't want to be overheard or disturbed.

CHAPTER 11

Logan was dozing when he felt someone touch his shoulder. He slowly opened his eyes and looked up. Henry was standing beside him, smiling.

"Sorry to interrupt you, sir, but you wanted me to let you know when we docked in Boston," Henry said. With his hands behind his back, he waited for Logan's response.

"Thank you, Henry. Could you tell one of the deckhands to take my bike out to the pier? I'll be down soon. Oh! And Henry, would you keep an eye on Precious while I'm out? Hopefully, I won't be too long," he said. He stretched his arms in the air, trying to wake up.

Henry nodded. "No, problem, I'd be delighted." Logan scanned the area for his puppy and spotted her immediately. She was napping on a cushion, on the floor near his chair. Henry scooped her up in his arms and stroked her head, talking to her sweetly as he disappeared from the deck.

Logan sat up on the edge of his chair and looked at his watch. It was ten minutes after three o'clock. He had slept a few hours. If he hurried, he should be able to catch Bailey before she finished her shift at the vet's clinic. He quickly headed to his stateroom to change his clothes. Arriving in Boston gave him joy in his heart.

He shed his clothes quickly and jumped into the shower. The hot water felt good on his body and it woke him up. He now was alert and ready to go find Bailey. He threw on a black pair of jeans and black t-shirt. He then slipped on a pair of black boots. He walked to the desk to search for Bailey's work address on his computer. He found it, wrote it down on a small piece of paper, and shoved it into his front pocket. He grabbed his leather jacket from the back of his chair and rushed out the door.

An hour later, he reached his destination. He parked his motorcycle at the curb, on the street. He took off his helmet and placed it on his handle bar. He took a long breath and let it out slowly. *What if she doesn't want to see me, or isn't happy about me showing up at her work place?* He couldn't think about it. He absolutely had to see her, so he could explain that it wasn't his fault and that he loved her. He leaped off his bike and headed to the clinic. He had to clear up this misunderstanding. He felt nervous, and his heart was beating fast against his chest as he approached the front door of the clinic.

He opened the door and stepped inside. His eyes surveyed the room. There was an empty waiting area to his right with framed pictures of animals on the walls. He noticed a reception section behind a glass window. He walked over to the woman who was sitting at the desk behind the glass. He waited for her to notice him while he looked around for Bailey. *She must be in the back.*

"Can I help you?" the receptionist asked him. Her tone wasn't friendly, as if she was annoyed at him. He altered his weight from one foot to another and asked pleasantly, "Hi, I'm a friend of Bailey's. Is she here? I'd like to have a word with her if possible."

The woman narrowed her eyes at him.

"No, she went home," she answered coldly and turned her attention back to her paperwork without another word. *What the hell was going on? Why was she avoiding him?* Stunned at her ill-mannered response toward him, he decided to try again.

"Excuse me, but would you have her home address? I really would like to see her," he asked politely with a small smile.

"I'm sorry, you will have to come back tomorrow. I can't give you her home address. It's against our policies. Is there anything else I can help you with?" she asked and sighed heavily. She seemed irritated that he was still there.

"No thank you, I'll come back tomorrow," he answered, turned and slowly walked out of the office. He was disappointed he had missed her. He wanted to hold her in his arms, smell her perfume and hear her laughter. He knew she lived in this town, but didn't have a clue exactly where. *What am I going to do? I don't even have her phone number. She left so abruptly. How am I going to find her?* He'd traveled so far to get here, and now he had to wait another day, another lonely night. He put on his helmet and mounted his motorcycle. He drove away back toward the yacht. Maybe she would be at the clinic tomorrow. *I will come back tomorrow. I will not give up so easily.*

***

Bailey sat on her couch in the living room looking out the window, daydreaming. She had arrived home a few hours previously, tossed her pocketbook aside on a chair and sat down heavily. She tried to analyze what had taken place at the restaurant. The unbelievable proposal Riker offered baffled her. *The only reason he would attempt to bribe me must be because Logan is near.*

She convinced herself Logan had to be here, but where would he be? How was he going to find her? She had never given him her home address. Why was Riker so against their relationship? A million questions passed through her brain without a decent answer to any of them. Why did Riker not want her to be with his brother? Was it just about her not being wealthy? She had other qualities. All she knew was she did love Logan, with all her being. If Logan came back to her, no one was ever going to put a wedge between them or tear them apart again. *The only thing I can do is wait. I hope Logan can find me. Riker hadn't had any difficulty locating me at the clinic.* She was confident Logan could track down the veterinary office.

Nightfall arrived at her doorstep so she decided to go to bed. She stood up and headed to her bedroom. She undressed, and slid into bed with a smile on her face. She had to get some sleep. Her mind kept going back to the time she'd spent with Logan. She would get up at dawn and be at work early. Finally, after tossing and turning for another half hour she fell into a deep sleep, anticipating the morning.

***

Riker was up even before the sun rose. He sat on his hotel room sofa for hours, debating what he should do about Bailey. He'd called one of his shady associates from New York, and requested that he send someone who had worked for him before, when he'd had trouble taking care of a problem. Someone reliable and efficient.

This woman's nickname was Ruby. Her name had been given to her because she was known for the red ruby lipstick that she always wore. She was a merciless person. She was a special private eye, with no guilt about what she had to do to achieve results—as long as she got paid the right amount. She had experience in many fields, but her specialty was analyzing her subjects, before she deceived them. Riker sent his private Gulfstream Aircraft to pick her up. He had been informed she had arrived safely before midnight and was staying in the same hotel, in room 790.

She was a high-priced contractor. Apparently she was worth every penny. She had never failed on her assignments since Riker had heard of her a few years back, from one of his colleagues. She was an ex-FBI operative, and profiler of psychological and behavioral characteristics.

She had left the bureau five years ago, after deciding she could make more money with her skills by servicing wealthy, private individuals.

She was well known for her stunning looks. She was a tall, lean woman, with waist-length black hair. She had lethal black eyes and high cheekbones that sent a chill down your back when she stared at you. People said she was a native Cherokee, but no one ever received a confirmation from her. She never backed away from her job until it was done.

Riker picked up his phone from the coffee table. He wanted to meet with this woman immediately. He dialed her private number. He brought the phone to his ear and waited with anticipation as he heard the first ring.

"Hello." Riker heard a female's voice answer on the other end of the line.

"Ruby, this is Riker. I'm sorry to call so early. Could we meet? I like to talk face to face," he asked.

The line was silent for a few seconds. Then he heard her say, "I'll be there in five minutes." The click told him she had hung up. Riker put the phone down and paused. He looked at his hotel door. He eagerly anticipated meeting this woman, and seeing what she could do. She came highly recommended.

Just a few minutes later, he heard a knock at his door. He stood and quickly walked to the door. He swung the door open and was face-to-face with an exquisite woman. She had to be at least six feet tall. She was dressed in a black leather bomber jacket, blue jeans, hiking boots, and a black toque that matched her black hair. She was carrying a leather backpack on her back. Her hands were tucked deep into her jacket pockets. He wondered if she was carrying a weapon. He instantly noticed her signature look; her full red lips. *Well, they were right!*

Ruby marched inside without saying a word. Riker closed the door behind her and followed her into the room. She stood erect, feet apart, and positioned herself by the large window that overlooked the Boston

Commons. She watched his every move with her eyes, not moving her head until he was a few feet from her. He extended his hand to shake her hand, but she rebuffed him by not taking her hands out of her jacket. She just lifted her eyebrows at him.

"Well, nice to finally meet you. Would you like something to drink?" Riker asked and pointed to the pot of coffee near them. She shook her head.

"Mr. St. James, I am here to deliver a service, not to chitchat and have coffee with you. Now please tell me what you would like me to do for you, and I'll tell you my price," she said emotionless. Her eyes fixed on him. He liked her. *She's cold! This might just work.*

"All right, I want you to break up my brother's love affair and make her think he's unfaithful. That's for starters; we can see how that works out. Do whatever is needed. The woman's name is Bailey Winters," he said, and reached for a folder that Blake Black had provided him. He picked it up and offered it to her.

"This is all the information I have on her and my brother Logan." She took a step forward and accepted the file from him. Riker watched as she read the first page, the next, and the next without saying a word. She lifted Bailey's picture and Logan's picture, peering at them. She seemed to be memorizing their features. She placed everything back in the folder, closed it, and gave it back to him.

"My fee is two hundred thousand dollars, because of certain risks that might occur," she said and placed her hands into her pockets once again.

"That's a lot of money. Are you sure you can..." she cut him off before he could finish.

"Do you want my services or not? I don't have time for games or negotiating," she threw a look at him and kept her eyes fixed on him.

"Fine, but you better be as good as they say," he replied. He turned around and walked to the side table in the bedroom. He pulled the drawer open and took out a thick envelope that contained cash. He walked back to the living room and stood facing her. He handed her the money.

"Half now, half when it is done. You'd better be worth it," he told her. He watched as she slipped the envelope into her pocket without counting it or even looking inside.

"I'll be in touch," she told Riker. She walked past him and marched out the door without another word.

***

Ruby walked out of Riker's room and headed for the entrance of the hotel. The first thing she had to do was rent a car, so she could follow and observe the targets. She had already done her research on the plane to Boston. She was always prepared. By all the gossip she had heard, she knew this situation probably had to do with his brother's love affair. She knew Riker didn't get along with Logan, and hadn't for years.

She made a beeline toward Boylston Street to the Enterprise Rent-a-Car. Within an hour she was out the door in a Lincoln SUV, and was driving toward the Boston Waterboat Marina on Long Wharf Street. That was where Logan's boat was docked. She quickly parked her SUV in the parking lot where she'd have a clear view of *The Vagabond*. She made herself comfortable, stretching out her legs, putting on her sunglasses, and waiting for Logan to appear. She unzipped her bag and retrieved her binoculars. She surveyed the area around the yacht. She noticed several crewmembers coming and going about their duties, but saw no sign of Logan. She saw a deckhand take out a motorcycle and place it on the pier.

An hour went by before she spotted Logan coming off his yacht. He was dressed in black jeans and a black leather jacket. He had a black helmet in his hand. He put it on, mounted his motorcycle, and drove away. She crouched down to avoid being detected. As soon as he passed her, she turned on the ignition of her vehicle and followed him at a safe distance.

He was going down the Massachusetts Turnpike, I-90 toward Newton. From what was written in Riker's file that was the area where Bailey worked. Ruby slowed down as she approached the clinic. This allowed Logan to turn in and park. She pulled over to the opposite side of the street, observing him as he took off his helmet and walked inside the vet's office. She couldn't see inside the office because the windows were too small and covered with curtains, so she would have to wait to see what happened. She couldn't take a chance of being discovered. She sat patiently, her eyes glued on the building for any movements.

Within minutes, Logan reappeared alone. He seemed disappointed, by his demeanor. He walked slowly back to his bike with his head bowed low and his shoulders slouched forward. He was shaking his head back and forth. She concluded Bailey wasn't there; or maybe she had rebuffed him.

Ruby started her SUV and followed Logan back to the dock. She parked her vehicle in the same spot as before. She watched him walk aboard the boat again and vanish.

She grabbed her phone and dialed the clinic. She had to find out if Bailey was at work or not. She heard the ringing and a young lady answered the phone, "Newton Veterinary Clinic, how may I help you?" she asked pleasantly.

"Good morning. Could I speak with Bailey Winters, please?" Ruby asked nicely.

"I'm sorry, but Bailey isn't here today. She's out sick, may I help you?" she replied. Ruby had her answer. She hung up the phone. Now she knew why Logan had left so quickly from the vet's office. *Bailey wasn't working today. Perfect!*

She reached inside her backpack and took out her computer. She opened it and tapped away at the keys. She ordered two bouquets of a dozen red roses, each from a nearby florist in Newton with a special note attached. She had one of them delivered to Bailey's home imme-diately. The other roses were delivered to Logan at his yacht. She had a lot of work to do. She started her SUV and drove in the direction of Bailey's house.

CHAPTER 12

Bailey's alarm clock rang. She could barely open her eyes to look at the time: seven o'clock. She pushed herself up. She sat with her head leaning against the headboard. A coldness ran through her body. Her head beat with pain. Her nose was stuffy and her throat was sore. She shoved the blankets off her and stood up. She suddenly felt dizzy, her head spinning. She had to sit down on the edge of her bed again. *Maybe I got up too fast.* She looked toward the bathroom cabinet, trying to recall what medicine she had for a cold. She slowly stood up and walked to the bathroom. She examined her face in the mirror, and noticed dark circles under her eyes. "What a day to get sick!" she said out loud. She reached up and opened the medicine cabinet. She shook two Tylenol Cold tablets out of the bottle into her left hand. She shuffled to the kitchen refrigerator, opened it, and grabbed the orange juice bottle. She poured herself a glass of juice and swallowed her pills with it.

I can't go to work like this. I can barely keep my head up. She made the decision she would take a sick day. She dragged herself back to bed with her drink in one hand and covered her body with the blanket. Another chill passed through her. She picked up her phone from her night table and called the office to tell them she wouldn't be in today. She lay her heavy head down on her pillow and closed her eyes, hoping that resting and drinking fluids would make her feel better. She quickly fell into a deep sleep as the cold medicine took effect.

A couple of hours later Bailey was awakened by the sound of the doorbell. Someone was at the front door. She rolled out of bed, grabbed her bathrobe and slipped it on as she walked toward the door. She glanced at the clock in the kitchen as she kept going forward. She noticed she didn't feel as sluggish, and her headache had subsided. As she approached the door she yelled out, "Who is it?" She looked into the peephole and saw a man in a uniform standing on the other side with flowers.

"Newton Florist," he answered.

Since she wasn't dressed and didn't know who they were from, she asked, "Could you leave them at the door, please?"

"Sure, no problem," he answered. She watched through the peephole as he bent down and placed the bouquet on her porch. He turned and walked away. She unlocked the doorknob and the opened the door. She picked up the arrangement of flowers and brought them to the counter in the kitchen. *What nice roses! I wonder who they're from?* She pondered as she searched for the card. She grasped it and read it. A wide smile appeared on her face, and all sickness faded away. It read:

Meet me,
Bar Boulud at the Mandarin Oriental Hotel, Boston
8:30 p.m. tonight
L SJ

Her heart skipped a beat. It was signed L SJ. *It had to be Logan.* He was in Boston. She knew he was coming and he had found her. She was right! Riker would not have offered her that money unless he knew Logan was in town. She couldn't wait to see him, and feel his muscular arms wrapped around her. She leaned forward to smell the roses. She closed her eyes as the aroma invaded her being. She missed him.

Nothing would keep her from this meeting tonight. He'd told her he loved her the day she left the yacht. Now she truly believed him. She felt the same. She pulled one of the roses from the vase. She brought it close to her chest as she inhaled the fragrance. She took the rose with her when she headed back to her bedroom, with Logan on her mind. She was excited, but she needed to lie down for another couple of hours. She hoped her cold would fade away. She contemplated the reunion. She was going to leap in his arms and kiss him like he had never been embraced before. She wanted to hold him against her warm body so she could feel every inch of him. She closed her eyes to reflect on how it was going to be with him in her life. Sleep invaded her senses and she dozed off with her future plans in tow.

***

Logan was disappointed that he had not been able to meet with Bailey. The girl at the desk would not give him her home address, even after telling her he was a friend. He had pleaded with her, but to no avail. He climbed on his bike and drove back to his boat. All the way back his thoughts were on Bailey. When he arrived on deck again he flopped into the chair at his desk, in his office. He couldn't believe he had traveled this far and still had to wait to feel her against his skin. He desperately wanted to hold her. There was nothing he could do, but bide his time until tomorrow. Hopefully she would be at the clinic then. He might as well keep his mind busy with work, so he concentrated on the legal agreements Riker had insisted he study and sign off on. He glanced at Precious, sleeping at his feet, a constant reminder of Bailey.

Logan was sitting at his desk reading over the contracts when he heard a knock on his door and looked up. It was mid-afternoon when Henry came to find him. Henry was the only one who would disturb him.

"Come in, Henry," he said. He watched Henry open the door and walk toward him, with a bouquet of roses in his hands. Logan creased his forehead as he watched Henry approach.

"These came for you. A delivery man from a local flower shop brought them in, sir," Henry told him and placed the roses on the edge of his desk. Henry turned and walked out, leaving Logan alone. Logan was surprised. *Who the hell would send me roses?* No one knew he was in Boston. He reached over and grabbed the card that was attached to one of the stems. He silently read the card. His mouth opened then turned into a full smile. It read:

Meet me,
The Harbor Sun Inn,
60 Main Street, Lexington, Mass.
5 p.m. today
B W

B W—it had to be Bailey! Someone at the clinic must have told her I was in town, but how did she find me? But if she knew where to send the roses, why didn't she come here? A million questions went through his mind, but he didn't care. All he knew was he was going to be reunited with his love. She had contacted him. He looked at his wrist watch. He had a few hours to wait before he was to go meet her. He was so excited. He kept singing a song while showering and getting dressed. He felt anxious and restless after he had dressed. He kept moving from one room to another, debating when to leave. He worried about being caught up in traffic and failing to be there on time. He didn't want to miss the reunion with his sweetheart. Finally he decided he would go early, and just wait for her at the inn.

Logan arrived at the inn around four fifteen in the afternoon and parked his Harley bike in the parking lot. He sat on his motorcycle for a moment, admiring the building. It seemed to shout Bailey to him. The outside of the Auberge was charming. It was a two-story, old-fashioned home that had a wraparound porch with double mahogany doors. It was painted in white and peach, with olive trim. It probably had been built in the late eighteen hundreds and the premises looked as if it had been completely refurbished to its original style. There were green bushes in the front and pots of yellow flowers hanging down from the porch's ceiling beams. It complimented the inn perfectly.

He walked up the steps to the veranda and into the entrance of the old colonial inn. He took two long strides forward and looked around. On his right there was a small, quaint pub area. It had a bar counter with six stools, and several tables in the back. He noticed a menu written on a huge blackboard attached to the wall, featuring comfort food like mac and cheese, burgers, and homemade soup. As he entered the bar he noted an antique wood stairway to the left, which probably led to the bedrooms upstairs. Every window in the bar area had some kind of stained glass that reflected rays of colorful sunshine into the room.

He could hear country music playing in the background as he sat down on the far side, at one of the tables by the window. He would be able to see Bailey when she arrived. The bartender smiled at him as she served drinks to the four patrons sitting in front of her at the counter. Logan figured he would be able to see everyone coming and going from his vantage point. He couldn't wait to see Bailey again. A rush of lust came to mind as he awaited her. He placed his hands on top of the table and read the menu on the wall. His stomach growled from hunger, and he remembered he hadn't had lunch. He had been too preoccupied with meeting Bailey to eat. He saw his server, wearing jeans with a white shirt and a short black apron, carrying a tray and walking towards him. She stopped next to his table.

"Hi, can I get you anything to drink or maybe to eat? The pasta is delicious!" she said with a smile. She looked down at him while holding her tray against her body.

"Sure, I'll have a Bud Light, and I'll try your lobster mac and cheese," he told her eyeing the door for Bailey.

"Great, I'll be right back," she said. She turned and walked away. She disappeared behind a door by the bar. Five o'clock came and went. Bailey had not shown up yet. Logan had eaten his meal and was on his second beer. His foot was tapping on the ground, his eyes darting around the room from nervousness wondering where Bailey could be. Something must have delayed her. He kept looking at his watch, and by five-thirty o'clock he was puzzled.

He wiped his hands over his face, worried that maybe she would not show. He was restless and kept squirming in his seat. He decided he would wait a little longer before he left the premises. He took another sip of his beer, then he saw a tall dark haired woman dressed in all black entering the pub. He watched her without moving his head. There was something about her that had caught attention. She glanced his way as she walked toward the bar area. She sat down at the counter and crossed her leg. She ordered a drink from the bartender, then rotated around on her seat to face him. She smiled his way. Logan looked away from her for a minute, not wanting to attract her attention. But when he peeked at her again, she was carrying two beers and was coming toward his table. She stopped, standing at the edge of his table. She placed one of the beers on his table in front of his beer, which was almost empty.

"Hi, I thought you might want another drink. Mind if I join you?" she asked, but didn't wait for an answer. She pulled out the chair next to him and sat down. Logan frowned at her. He hadn't told her she could have a seat, and he was annoyed.

"I'm meeting someone. I'd rather wait alone," he told her, as he watched her take a drink from her beer.

"Well, I'll tell you what, I'll keep you company until whoever you are meeting arrives. Then I'll leave, okay?" she said and smiled at him once again. Logan didn't know what to say. He was caught by surprised at her suggestion. She was so forward and blunt.

Logan just nodded slightly and said, "Fine." Logan turned his sight toward the entrance and tried to ignore her.

"My name is Sandra, what's yours?" she asked him nicely.

Without looking at her he answered, "Logan."

"I noticed you were almost done with your beer so I brought you another one," she said. Logan still didn't pay her any attention. He didn't turn to her or acknowledge her.

"Hey! Listen, I'm just being friendly. I'm just killing time, like you. I'm also meeting my better half, and I thought we could talk until they arrived. You don't have to be rude," she told him softly. He turned to face her, feeling a bit guilty that he was so impolite. *I suppose it would be all right that she might distract me until Bailey walks in.*

"I'm sorry, thank you for the beer," he told her. He reached for his beer and gulped down the last drops of it.

"Who are you waiting for?" he asked her, as she pushed the fresh beer toward his hand.

She lifted her beer and took a sip. "I'm waiting for my husband. He's supposed to meet me here after work. We're going to have dinner. What about you?" she asked, and smiled at him again.

Logan sighed in relief that she was married and would be departing soon. He reached over with his right hand and grasped the beer she had bought him. He lifted the mug to his lips and swallowed a mouthful.

"Thanks! I'm expecting my girlfriend, Bailey. I presume your husband isn't a jealous man, when you go sit with strange men while expecting him," Logan said trying to get information from her.

"Not at all, he trusts me," she answered and laughed a little. She lifted her drink up for a toast and clicked her rim on his drink.

"Here's to our better halves," she said, and took another sip. Logan took his drink and did the same, taking a slug of his beer. Logan raised his wrist once again to look at his watch. Bailey was extremely late. *Something was not right.*

"Something wrong?" he heard her ask. He shook his head. He found his head suddenly felt heavy. He blinked several times, trying to clear his vision. His vision was a bit blurry, but he concluded it must be the alcohol.

"No, no, I'm okay," he answered. Feeling unstable, he shook his head slightly.

"Drink up then," she told him, drinking more of her beer. He took another sip of his beer. Ten minutes passed. His speech slurred when he tried to talk. He was feeling very tired, and could barely keep his eyes open. He had almost emptied his beer and he felt drunk. *How many beers did I have?* The room started to spin. *Why am I sitting in this bar?* He felt dizzy.

"Something isn't right..." Logan could barely speak, much less move. His mouth was like sandpaper.

"Why don't you take my arm, and come lay down for a while? I have a room near by. You've had too much to drink. Come on, let's go." He heard the words, but didn't know who it was. He could barely understand what was being said to him. He could feel someone's arm around his waist, lifting him off his seat. *Bizarre!* He was confused. He was standing, but didn't know where he was going. *Something definitely was wrong.* He noticed he was in a bedroom. He felt like he was floating, and it seemed that he was dragging his feet. Everything went blank.

***

Bailey felt much better when she woke up from her afternoon nap. She had slept for almost four hours. She stretched her arms and rubbed her eyes. Her nose wasn't stuffy any longer and the pain in her throat had disappeared. She glanced at her alarm clock on her nightstand. It was five o'clock. She still had plenty of time to shower, get dressed, and arrive at Boulub on time. She pushed away the blanket and went to the kitchen. The flowers made her heart skip a beat. Twice he had sent her flowers. She smiled.

She walked over and cupped the flowers in her hands, inhaled deeply and smelled their fragrance. She decided she shouldn't go out to meet Logan on an empty stomach, so she placed two pieces of bread in the toaster. She ate quickly, then headed toward the bedroom to get ready for her meeting with Logan. From her closet, she picked a light blue outfit that accentuated her curves. She applied lipstick, sprayed a touch of fragrance on and brushed her long black hair. She took one last look in the mirror and was satisfied. She left the house, eager to go meet her love.

The taxi driver dropped her off in front of the Mandarin Hotel on Boylston Street, where the bar was located. She paid the cabbie and step out of the cab. She pushed open the glass entrance door to the building. Bailey stood in the lobby for a minute, surveyed the area, trying to orient herself. The lobby was bustling with people coming and going, either registering or leaving the hotel. A couple of older women being served cocktails were sitting at table on her right on one of the brown couches. Bailey followed the server with her eyes, and saw the entry of the bar. *Perfect!*

She slowly walked toward the entrance of Boulud. She admired the curved teak beams on the ceiling and the arches that surrounded the red velvet booths overlooking the street outside. She saw a long bar with high stools on the left, so without deviating from her stride, she went to the counter. She pulled out the high chair and sat down, crossed her legs and looked at the variety of bottles of alcohol in front of her.

She ordered a glass of white wine and tried to relax while waiting for Logan. She drank her wine slowly and munched on a bowl of nuts the bartender set in front of her. She kept checking the entryway, hoping to spot Logan, but forty minutes later he still hadn't arrived at Boulud. Bailey's nerves were thin and she was restless. She played with her napkin, folding and unfolding it. She swallowed the last drop of her wine. She placed her hands on her knee, which had started to jiggle lightly from nervousness. Fear swept over her. *What if he doesn't show?* She bit her lower lip, wondering where he could be.

"Would you like another glass of wine?" she heard the bartender ask. He reached for her empty glass.

"Sure," she answered. Bailey watched him pour her another glass of Pinot noir. She looked at her watch as the minutes flew by. It was now eight fifteen. She played different scenarios in her mind to explain why he was late, wondering if he would even show. Maybe his motorbike broke down, or maybe there was a lot of traffic, or maybe he had gotten sick. She was really worried. She was now biting her fingernails.

She felt embarrassed that she was still sitting at the bar at nine o'clock, alone. He had not shown; he failed to keep his date. She gulped the last of her wine. She felt sad. She bowed her head, having been duped into believing he cared for her. If he did care, he wouldn't have left her hanging. She was about to leave when a young man came forward. He stood next to her chair. She turned toward him and gave him a weak smile. Bailey stood up and was about to leave the bar when she heard him say, "Excuse me, are you Bailey Winters?"

She noticed he was holding a large yellow envelope in his hand. She looked at him and answered, "Yes." She was puzzled. *What does this guy want from me? How did he know my name? Logan must have sent him.*

"This is for you," he said. He handed the envelope to her and quickly walked away. *Weird!* She watched him exit the bar. She looked down at the envelope in her hands. There was no writing on it. It was just a large, yellow envelope. *Who sent this to me? It has to be from Logan. No one else knows where I am.* She decided to take it to the lobby, because the bar was getting crowded and she didn't want anyone looking over her shoulder. She took out a ten and a twenty from her clutch and placed them under her empty wine glass.

Bailey almost ran out of the bar, headed toward the lobby. She found an empty chair in a private corner and sat down. She looked around before she opened the back of the envelope and put her hand inside. She pulled out a bunch of pictures. Immediately her hands started to shake uncontrollably as she viewed the photos. She could barely hold on to the photographs. Her heartbeat started to race. Her eyes were burning from the tears. She tried to gain control of her emotions. She shoved everything back inside the envelope and surveyed the lobby for the young man, but he was nowhere to be seen. She must have sat immobile for ten minutes. She couldn't move. She gripped the envelope tightly between her fingers until she realized she couldn't stay here. She stood up and blindly walked to the entrance. Even the fresh air of the night didn't help her trembling body. She hailed a cab at the curb of the hotel and left as swiftly as she could to return home.

CHAPTER 13

Later in the evening, around eleven o'clock, Riker sat in one of the chairs in his suite at the hotel. He was studying contracts from his company when he was interrupted by a knock on the door. He glanced at on his Rolex watch, on his left wrist. He frowned and placed his documents on the coffee table in front of him. He stood and walked over to open the door, wondering who would be disturbing him at this late hour. When he opened the door, there stood Ruby. She walked past him without a word. He noticed she was carrying a large envelope in one hand. He closed the door quickly and went to join her in the living room area.

She stood erect in a military stance, one hand tucked away in her pocket and the other holding a large yellow envelope. Riker moved nearer to her and she extended her hand toward him with the package.

"I took these photographs and they were delivered to Miss Winters. And judging by her reaction, she didn't seem pleased. I don't think you will have any more problems with her," Ruby announced. She waited, expressionless, her eyes observing his every move. Riker took out the pictures in the envelope and examined each one. He smirked at her in triumph and put the photos back into the envelope.

"Nice work," a gleeful sound escaped from Riker as he threw them on the coffee table in front of him.

"I do believe we are done. I won't need your services any longer," he told her, heading toward the desk. He bent down, grabbed his leather satchel from beside the desk, and took out a stack of hundred dollar bills bound with a currency band. He walked back, turned to her until they were face-to-face, and handed her the money.

"It's been a pleasure," Riker said. She took the bundle of bills and placed it in an inside pocket of her jacket without counting it.

"Thank you. Until next time," she told him, as she moved past him with long strides. She disappeared behind the hotel door without another word. Riker was left standing alone in the living room. He heard the door shut.

He took two steps to his right and retuned to his original spot. He sat down, reached over and grabbed his business agreements in his hand, but suddenly stopped before he continued reading the contracts. His sight was drawn to the yellow envelope that lay on the coffee table. He couldn't help himself. He smiled. It was just too much! He laughed out loud. *Bailey and Logan are no longer a couple.*

He was sure that he had gotten rid of Bailey. She would refuse Logan now. He tapped his index finger on his mouth. He had to do whatever was necessary to keep the integrity of the future of the family. He was the head of this family, and he believed he had spared his brother a major hardship. Logan may have been humiliated a little by the situation, but he would get over it. He could now return to New York without any worries or distractions from that woman. He picked up his papers and snickered to himself as he started reading the documents.

***

Logan opened his eyes and quickly realized he was alone. *Where am I?* The room had multicolored, flowered wallpaper and a picture of countryside scenery. He was in a four-poster bed in someone's bedroom, but whose? His head was hurting. His temples were throbbing with the utmost discomfort. He grimaced, in extreme pain. He could barely keep his eyes focused. He propped up on his elbows and inspected the room a little more closely by slowly moving his head from side to side, scanning the bedroom. *Where the hell am I?*

It was unrecognizable. He suddenly realized what looked like his shirt and pants lay on a chair next to the door. He could see a bathroom on his left. He pushed the blanket off his body and his eyes bulged out. He swallowed hard. He was shocked to find out he had no clothes on. He was completely naked. "What the fuck?" he heard himself say out loud. He sat at the edge of the bed and placed his hands on the sides of his head, with his elbows on his knees. He closed his eyes for a moment. He needed to orient himself. He opened his eyes, stood, and walked directly to his clothes. He quickly got dressed. He hurried toward the door, opened it, and realized he was at the inn.

Bits and pieces rushed back to him. *I was at the bar and I felt sick. That woman with the black hair must have brought me here.* He wasn't drunk, because he'd only had three beers while he waited for Bailey. *Bailey hadn't showed; or had she?* He couldn't recall. He was fine until that woman bought him his last beer. He remembered her taking him away from the table when he didn't feel well. *Who was she? What had he done? What had happened last night?* He couldn't recall and his mind was playing tricks on him. He had to find out who this woman was, because she had the answer to all his questions.

Logan made his way outside. He leaned one hand against the railing of the porch for minute, trying to remember how he had ended up in a strange bedroom. The fresh air helped as he inhaled deeply. He needed to find out what had happened to him. He saw his bike was still parked in the nearby parking lot. He scurried to it, put his helmet on and took off in the direction of his yacht.

Logan was not a patient man when he boarded *The Vagabond*. He marched straight to his stateroom, bypassing the deck crew without any greetings except for screaming, "Where is Henry? I want to see Henry immediately. Someone find him!" He entered his bedroom and slammed the door. He paced back and forth in his room, breathing very hard. He heard a knock on his door.

"Come in," he shouted.

Henry came forward with his hands outstretched and an expression of concern on his face, his eyes wide with worry. "Are you okay, Logan? You seem agitated. Did something happen? Bailey?"

Henry took Logan's arm and motioned for him to sit down. Henry sat beside him on the sofa. He touched Logan's shoulder softly with his hand and said, "Calm down, Logan."

Logan could feel himself relaxing and nodded at him.

"Now, you know I love you like my own son, so tell me from the beginning what has happened to perturb you so. Maybe I can help," Henry said in quiet voice.

"Henry, I'm not sure what happened. One minute I was at the Harbor Sun Inn, waiting for Bailey to arrive. She never showed. I waited for her for hours. A tall black-haired woman came to sit with me. She brought me a beer. The next thing I knew, I woke up this morning in a bedroom, naked and I...I can't remember much after that last beer... nothing," Logan's voice broke and he dropped his head in his hands. He wanted to cry. He was not going to let Henry see how upset he was. Henry didn't say anything for a minute. He seemed to be thinking.

"You were probably drugged. She dropped a roofie in your drink. It takes effect within fifteen minutes, and your memory becomes impaired afterwards. The question is who was the woman? And what did she want from you?" Henry reached over and gently rubbed Logan's back.

"It will be all right. I will find the missing pieces. I promise you. Now, go take a long shower. I'll make some calls and check some things out for you, okay?" Henry said.

"You think someone drugged me? Why?" Logan whispered to Henry.

"I really don't know why, but I will find out. Don't worry; let me probe around, okay?" Henry marched to the door and turned to look at him.

"Henry, take whatever money you need from the safe, and be careful. I'll be here. Thank you for helping and being my friend," Logan told him. Logan stood and headed for the bathroom. A weight had been lifted from his shoulders. The only thing he had on his mind now was finding Bailey.

***

Henry exited the stateroom with his hands balled into fists. He was furious someone had taken advantage of Logan. *He was such a harmless soul! Who would do such a thing to him?* He had a feeling...no, it was more than a feeling. He would bet his life that Logan's brother Riker had something to do with what happened to Logan. He would be the only one who detested him enough to drug him so he couldn't meet with Bailey. Henry knew how Riker operated. He was a conniving, underhanded bastard, and most of all, selfish. Riker had always been jealous of his younger brother's easygoing attitude.

Henry went directly to his room and changed into a white shirt and black trousers. He had a private informer, Carol, who worked closely in the brothers' company and had worked closely with Riker for years. She was one of Riker's private assistants. She always had been loyal to Logan, even after the brothers split and had gone their separate ways. She really didn't like the way Riker treated his brother, so she had continually come through with information or whatever was going on with Riker. Henry paid her very well for her services, so it worked out great for both of them.

The first thing Henry decided to do was go to the inn and find out if there was a way to identify the woman who had been in the bar with Logan. He walked down to the end of the dock and hailed a cab to take him to the inn in Lexington. He was dropped off in front of the building within the hour.

"Could you wait for me? I shouldn't be too long," Henry said to the cab driver.

"No problem. But could you pay me the fare you owe me so far?" he asked Henry, looking at him in the rearview mirror. Henry took out his wallet from his back pocket and handed the man a one hundred dollar bill.

"Will that do?" Henry asked him and pushed the door open..

"Yes, that will do just fine. I'll be here, take your time," the driver answered, taking the money from Henry.

Henry walked up to the front door and entered the lobby. He looked to his right and continued toward the bar area. His eyes caught sight of a black, rounded dome, mounted on the wall behind the counter in the corner of the bar. He had also noticed another camera was installed near the front entrance. He concluded a security system was present. He approached the counter to talk to the bartender. He was hopeful that he could obtain an image of the woman. He stopped at the counter waited for the bartender to make his way toward him. The establishment was empty, except for one couple having a late breakfast.

"Good morning, what can I get you?" the bartender asked as he placed a napkin in front of Henry.

"Well, I was wondering if I could speak to the owner or the manager," Henry asked, smiling.

"Sure, let me check to see if he's available. I'll be right back," he told him. He turned and disappeared down a small corridor in the back area of the bar. Henry pulled out a stool and sat down, awaiting the manager. A man in his late forties wearing a dark blue shirt and black pants came forward to Henry and said, "Hi, I'm the owner. How can I help you?" Henry replied quietly, not wanting to be overheard.

"Good afternoon, sir. An incident happened last evening that would not be to your advantage if it were known. I would like to inquire about the type of security system you have at this inn, and whether or not it recorded the incident last night. My employer is trying to find out who this person might have been, or if you would have a photograph of this individual on film," Henry explained.

"Are you with the police?" the owner asked with a concerned look.

"No, I'm not," Henry answered.

"Well, first I would have to know what kind of incident you are talking about." he told Henry. At that moment Henry decided to speak in an even more hushed tone. He stood up and leaned closer to the ear of the owner.

"My employer is a very prominent and discreet person. He believes this person drugged him last night in your establishment, and we are trying to find her. We would like to acquire the CD. You wouldn't want to have bad publicity, so he is willing to compensate you for your time and confidentiality." Henry took out five hundred dollar bills that were folded in two and placed it on the counter in front of the man. The owner eyed the money in front of him. He pushed the money back with his hand toward Henry.

"First, let's see what we have. I will help, but you don't have to pay me. I don't want your money." Henry covered the cash with his hand and placed it back to his pocket.

"First, l am sorry if it did happen and I'll be glad to assist if I can. Please, follow me," he told Henry and signaled him to follow. Henry trailed the owner closely as he walked to a small office, a ten by twelve room with a small window. There was a wooden chair at a matching desk with a pile of papers, two guest chairs that faced the desk, and two filing cabinets. On a shelf to his left were two monitors, showing the bar area and the entrance of the inn. Henry observed that a date and time were marked on the right hand corner of the image.

"If you would like to have a seat, I'll rewind the CD so we can see what we have, all right?" the man asked. But Henry didn't budge from where he was standing, with his arms folded in front of his chest. His eyes were on the monitors.

"Sir, I would rather just buy the CD from you. My employer is very private, and doesn't want to be recognized or have the incident known. I am willing to pay you one thousand dollars for the CD of yesterday evening. Otherwise he might take legal action against your establishment for negligence, and believe me, you would not want that," Henry said in a serious tone. Henry noticed the owner seemed nervous. He was rubbing his hands together as he walked to the monitors. He pushed a button to eject the CD. He reached over and put it into a plastic sleeve. Henry extended his hand to accept the CD. He waited with a blank expression on his face.

"Your boss won't bother us or sue us if I give it to you, right? I don't want any trouble. Correct?" he asked with uncertainty. Henry saw droplets of sweat forming on his brows.

"That is correct." Henry waited patiently, with his hand still outstretched. He placed the CD into Henry's palm. Henry put it in his inside jacket pocket. He reached into his pants pocket and took out a large roll of hundred dollars bills. The owner took a step back as his mouth twisted slightly, but not a sound erupted. Henry counted ten bills and dropped it on the desk.

"For your cooperation and inconvenience," Henry said. He turned on his heel and walked out the same way he had entered, without another word to the owner. Henry went back to his taxi and left the inn.

Henry was back on the yacht within an hour. He walked straight to Logan's office. He had just inserted the CD into his computer when Logan strolled in. He came forward to stand beside Henry.

"I retrieved last night's security footage from the inn," he told Logan. He clicked the play button and forwarded to the approximate time when she'd walked into the bar. They watched as the bartender served her two beers. There it was. They observed her dropping a pill in one of the beers. She wandered to his table, sat down and pushed the beer toward Logan. Logan turned his head to look away. He was stunned. He raked his hand through his curls. He walked over to the large window and stared out at the ocean. Henry could tell he was hurting, by the way he shook his head and walked away from the screen. Henry stopped the CD and printed a picture of her face. He forwarded a duplicate to his phone so he could send it to Carol. He was hoping that Carol might know of this woman.

"Why do you think she did it? I don't even remember what happened after..." he questioned and turned to look at Henry. Henry just shrugged, not wanting to let him know his thoughts until he was certain it was Riker's doing.

"Logan, just give me a little time. I will find the answers. I promise," he told Logan and patted him on the shoulder for encouragement. Logan closed his eyes and just nodded at him. Leaving Logan alone, Henry marched out of the room to go work on his sources.

***

By noon Logan was feeling better. At least his head wasn't throbbing as it had when he woke up that morning. He lay down on his bed to take a nap, but suddenly the bed felt empty and frosty without Bailey by his side. He decided not to fret over it, so, he got up, took a shower, and had the chef prepare him a hearty breakfast of eggs and bacon with potatoes. He sat at the small dining table outside on the back deck. Logan looked around in the vicinity of the pier, observing the people sauntering along the dock and admiring the boats.

He could smell the ocean breeze and he could see the other boaters' comings and goings. He closed his eyes and relaxed, extending his legs under the table as he felt the sun warm his body. His reverie shifted to Bailey. He desperately needed to see her. He had traveled so far to find her, and that was what he was going to do. He had to get over this trauma of being drugged and go find her. *Henry will take care of every-thing. He will find the culprit, and all my questions will be answered.* He had complete faith in Henry, because he had never let him down before.

He looked at the clock on the wall; it was now eleven in the morning. If he hurried, he might be able to catch Bailey at the office and take her to lunch. He threw his napkin on the table and with a quick pace headed off the yacht to get on his motorcycle. He placed his helmet on his head and attached the strap. He mounted his bike, turned the key, and took off in the direction of the clinic to go find Bailey. As he drew near the clinic, he saw a woman walking down the sidewalk. He knew from the way her hips moved from side to side and her long hair bounced on her shoulders, it was Bailey. He would recognize her walk anywhere. She was in her uniform, walking down the street, holding a take-out Chinese food bag.

Logan pulled his bike closer to the curb and dropped his feet to the ground so he could hold his bike upright while still rolling in her direction. He was about twenty feet away. He opened his glass visor with hand and whistled at her, but she kept going. He did it again, but this time much louder. Bailey slowed down and turned her head in his direction. She looked straight at him with an expression of revulsion and moved her nose upward at him. He gave her a wide smile and waved at her, but she didn't reciprocate the gesture. She felt her lips tighten and her eyes narrowed at him. She was mad at him, but Logan didn't know why she would be angry. She ignored him. She quickened her pace and kept looking straight ahead without acknowledging him.

Logan was confused. *Why isn't she happy to see me? Why is she fuming at me? She seems to be avoiding me.* He parked his bike immediately and swiftly dismounted. He rushed toward her. He unstrapped his helmet and took it off while dashing in her direction.

"Bailey, Bailey stop! It's me, Logan," he yelled. She kept rushing away from him. Logan finally gently grabbed her forearm to make her stop moving away.

"Bailey what's the matter? Aren't you happy to see me? I missed you so much," he said. He saw an expression of disgust on her face. She turned away and looked down at his hand on her arm. She briskly pulled away from his contact as if he had burned her.

"Let go of me! Stay away from me. I don't want to have anything to do with you, you bastard!" she yelled at him. She stood her ground. Puzzled by her reaction, he couldn't move for an instant. His eyebrows came together; he was confused.

"What? Why?" he asked. He saw tears building in her eyes. *Why was she crying? What does she think I did?* She didn't respond to him. She took a step forward and continued on her way. Logan stood rooted in his spot. He watched her walk away from him.

"Bailey, I don't know what you're talking about. I wouldn't hurt you. Please, talk to me," he yelled, but she didn't stop. She just hurried on her way and disappeared around the corner of the building, leaving him alone on the sidewalk. He had so many questions without answers.

He bent his head down, devastated she had rebuffed him. He turned around, put his helmet back on, and went back to his motor-bike. He didn't understand her reaction. *What does she think I've done? Why wasn't she delighted to see me?* He had traveled across an ocean to see her again. He didn't know, but he would find out. He wasn't going to give up on her so easily. *It probably has to do with last night, or maybe Riker said something to her. But he isn't in Boston, or is he?* Logan hopped on his bike and returned to his ship.

CHAPTER 14

Bailey arrived back at the vet's office after picking up lunch down the block. She was flustered. Her cheeks were pink and her hair was unkempt from twirling strands between her fingers as she tried to get away from Logan. He'd appeared out of nowhere. As soon as she made the corner of the building, she lost it. She couldn't breathe, and her throat was slowly closing. She was having a panic attack. She bent over, trying to get air back into her lungs. It took her a few minutes, but finally it passed, and she continued on her way with tears blurring her sight.

She placed the bag of food on the table in the lunchroom and was thankful she was alone. She noticed her hands were still shaking from the encounter and stuffed them in her pockets. Her heart was racing. She pulled out a chair and sat, trying to calm down. *He was here!* She had been right all along, but seeing him in person made it real.

She thought back to what he'd told her. *How dare he come around, after the pictures I saw of him last night? Did he think I was going to be one of his little companions, his playmates, who would just jump every time he snapped his fingers or breezed through town? Oh, no!* Bailey looked at the bag on the table. She'd lost her appetite. She reflected on the brief conversation that had taken place on the street. *He didn't know what I was mad about?*

Ha! I never want to see him again. Suddenly, she felt tightness in her chest. A wave of anguish passed through her again. *He betrayed me! How dare he think I would take him back, after such disloyalty?* She didn't need this. She was a strong woman, and she would have to move on with her life without him. *What he did was unforgivable! I couldn't live with the uncertainties! He might find another woman to be with.* Her eyes burned as she put her hands in front of her face and wept silently.

***

Riker flew back to New York on his private jet the following morning. His chauffeur picked him up at the Newark Airport hanger and drove him to Park Avenue in Manhattan by early afternoon. He was now sitting behind a large mahogany desk on the thirty-third floor of the Seagram Building. A painting by Picasso hung on the wall across from his desk. There was a glass bar to his right that held a single-malt whiskey collection. He loved his office. It was a grand place, with a sitting area that consisted of two white leather couches with a large square coffee table between them, and a conference room to his left that was enclosed with glass doors.

Riker was relaxing in his chair, facing the floor to ceiling windows which featured unmatchable views of Park Avenue and the many skyscrapers of the city. He was holding a crystal cut tumbler in his right hand. It contained a double shot of twenty-six year-old Glenfiddich. He was celebrating the break-up, because of his brother's misadventure of the previous night. He brought the alcohol to his nose, smelled it, swirled it in his glass and sipped it slowly. He was enjoying his devious victory.

His family had rented the whole thirty-third floor since the building was first built, in 1958. This was his empire. He felt powerful here in this office, overseeing his staff. People would tremble and run when he spoke to them, unlike his brother, who never listened to him.

Riker's thoughts drifted back to when he went to meet Logan on his yacht in the Caribbean. He twitched his nose and pressed his lips together as if there was something repugnant in the air. *Well, Logan will regret the day he told me to leave his yacht. I have been humiliated for the last time. I am in charge as the head of this family, and I will bring my wrath down on him. He will listen to me from now on.* He laughed out loud.

He spun his chair around and placed his drink on his desk. He still had a smile on his face. He had taken care of the problem with Logan; he was sure Bailey wouldn't have anything to do with Logan now. It was early, so he decided to catch up on his workload. He was behind on things since he had been gone for a number of days. He opened one of his folders and was studying certain spreadsheets of financial matters when his secretary interrupted him by buzzing his phone.

"Mr. St. James, there's a woman here without an appointment, by the name of Ruby. She won't give me her last name, and she demands to see you. Would you like me to bring her to your office?" she asked.

"Yes, show her in," Riker said. He was annoyed that she had shown up at his office before calling him. He did not want to meet with her at this office. He reached over for his drink and swallowed the last mouthful. He made a grimace because of the burning going down to his stomach. He stood up and walked to the other end of the room to position himself by the window. He placed his knuckles on his hips as he admired the view and waited for her. He was irritated because he wanted to keep their dealings secretive, and didn't want to be seen or associated with this woman. He also knew why she was there.

He heard a knock on the door and he answered, "Enter." He heard the door open and the footsteps coming into his office. He listened until the door of his office was shut before he turned around to face Ruby. He narrowed his eyes at her, looking at her closely before he spoke to her. She was dressed in all black, standing by his desk in her usual military stance, hands clasped behind her back. *She looks beautiful, but deadly.* He walked around the desk over to her without taking his eyes off her. He stopped, bent down to open one of the desk drawers, and took out an envelope. She didn't move, but her eyes were on him. He threw it on the top of the desk just a few inches from the edge.

"I thought you would contact me beforehand, not just show up at my office," he said harshly. She didn't respond right away, she just lifted her eyebrows as her forehead creased.

"That's your problem. Next time pay me what you owe me. You cheated me of almost half what we had agreed on. That was a sly move, holding my money until I delivered my services," she replied calmly. Riker heard a half-suppressed laugh from her, but without any kind of movement. Riker's patience was being tested, but it didn't seemed to bother her. He inhaled deeply, then clenched his teeth and exhaled through his nose. He leaned his body forward, placing his palms on the top of his desk.

"You don't have any sense of humor," he laughed.

"There won't be a next time. Take your money and leave, now." He raised his voice in a somewhat impatient tone. Riker clamped his jaw, not wanting to say anything else. She took a step forward and picked up the envelope. She didn't bother to count the cash. She unzipped her jacket and placed the envelope in an inside pocket. She re-zipped her jacket, never taking her eyes of him. She tilted her head at him and said, "It's been a pleasure, but don't ever think to cheat me because I will find you. Thank you."

Riker formed two fists as he scowled her way. She took a step back, turned toward the exit and strutted her stuff out the door, leaving it open as she continued to walk away. "Damn that fucking woman!" Riker said under his breath. He observed Carol, one of his assistants, closing the door. He sat down again, grabbed a folder and went back to work as if nothing had transpired in the office. He was glad he would not be teaming up with Ruby again.

***

Henry sat at his desk in his room on the yacht, making numerous calls to his connections who might have information on this woman. He determined, by the way she orchestrated the events and had access to the drug that she was a professional. He also noted on the film that a second woman departed the inn about the same time as Ruby. She didn't look as lethal or as classy as Ruby. She looked out of place at the inn, in the mini dress she wore and her high platform heels. She was the best lead he had. She was Asian and, by her attire, she was probably from the Chinatown area.

He monitored the other patrons of the evening and determined she had to be a hired hand. He would have bet his life she was a hooker from the downtown streets. He went to the printer, pressed the on button, and returned to his computer. He pressed the enter key on his computer to print pictures of both women. He folded them and stuck them in his pants pocket.

He only had one more person to contact. This person worked in close proximity with Riker. Henry looked at his watch. It was now half past five o'clock. She should be done with work by now. He didn't want to disrupt her at her place of employment and risk that she would be overheard, or worse, bump into Riker. He dialed her cellphone number and waited as it rang. She answered, "Hello?"

"Hi Carol, this is Henry, how have you been?" he asked pleasantly. He studied the picture of the woman with long black hair.

"I'm fine. What about yourself?" she inquired pleasantly.

"Everything is okay. Are you able to talk privately at this moment?" he asked. He wanted to make sure she wasn't still at work and was alone.

"Yes, I'm at home. By the way, how is Logan? I miss him," she answered.

"He's in a little bind. That's what I wanted to talk to you about. First, do you know if Riker is in New York?" he asked casually.

"Yes. As a matter of fact, he just got back this afternoon. I think someone said he was in Boston on business," she answered, unaware of anything that had happened to Logan.

"Do you know how long he was in Boston, and for what reason?" Now Henry had some information on Riker's whereabouts in the past few days. He was right.

"I was told he went somewhere in the Caribbean Islands for a few days to visit Logan, but from what I understood from his secretary Doreen, he flew to Boston afterwards," she informed him.

"I want you to try and remember if at any time since he has been back in New York, did you see a tall woman with long black hair around the office?" he asked, hoping she could help him.

"As a matter of fact, yes. There was a tall woman with long black hair in the office today, and Riker was not in a good mood when she arrived unannounced. Doreen told me that," she said.

"Carol, listen very carefully. I'm going to send you two pictures and I need you to tell me if you recognize them, okay? I need to know if the woman with the black hair you saw today is the same one." Henry pressed buttons on his phone and transmitted the photographs to her.

"Let me know when you receive them. I'll wait," he said. He patiently stood and looked out his cabin window, anticipating a response. He held on to his phone tightly. He was sure he was on the right track. Riker was the culprit of this incident, and all he had to do was prove it.

"Henry, that's her, the lady with the black hair from this afternoon. The other one I don't know. I overheard her name was Ruby. I remember, because she wouldn't give Riker's secretary her last name. I overheard Doreen insisting, but the woman just repeated her name was Ruby, like red."

"Carol, do you know what she wanted?" he asked. He was elated he had a name.

"No, I couldn't hear much, except Riker told her something about taking the money and to leave his office," she said.

"You are a doll, and very helpful. Please don't forget to delete the photos. You shall be rewarded and, as usual, let's keep this between us," he said. He was ecstatic about all he had heard. He now knew her name, and he was sure Riker had paid her.

"Thanks Henry. Anything for Logan! Hug him for me. Bye," she said, then Henry heard the line go dead. He smiled as he looked his phone. He had a solid lead to work with, and that was all he needed.

Within seconds he was off the yacht and sitting in the back of another taxi, going to downtown Boston to meet up with another friend, who also might be able to help him. His destination was in an area known as the red-light district of Chinatown. It was located at the edge of downtown Boston's shopping and financial district.

He was hopeful someone in the massage-parlor industry would be able to identify the Asian woman. First he had to convince them to talk to him; otherwise he was dead in the water. He was going to meet with Miss Yang, an acquaintance of a colleague he'd contacted earlier in the day. He was told this lady owned several escort services, but they were actually a front for prostitution in Chinatown.

She was expecting Henry, and she would be willing to provide information for a fee. The meeting was planned to take place at The China Pearl restaurant, located on Tyler Street in Chinatown.

"You can drop me off at the Chinatown Opening Gate," Henry told the driver as he approached the Chinese architectural Paifang-style gate on Beach Street.

"No problem," he answered and pulled to the curb. Henry took out cash from his pocket and gave him a thirty dollars through the opening in the cab's glass between the front and back seats. Henry reached for the handle and opened the door. He stepped out and immediately walked toward the entrance of Chinatown.

Tyler Street wasn't far, so Henry decided to stretch his legs and walk down Beach Street. He loved all the Chinese signs depicting the many restaurants, markets, and oriental stores that lined the street. The Asian culture was alive in this little corner of the city. He heard several different Oriental dialects being spoken. The bright colors of red, orange, and yellow lined the many storefronts of the street. The aroma of the food traveled in the air and tantalized his nose. He arrived at the corner and turned left on Tyler Street, where he would meet Miss Yang. The restaurant was on the right, about a block up from his position. He noticed the yellow neon sign above the entrance, pushed open the door, and entered. A young Asian lady greeted him.

"Good afternoon, how many?" she asked in a thick accent.

"I'm meeting a friend. Her name is Miss Yang, and she said she would make reservations," he answered.

"Oh yes, Miss Yang, come with me," she told him, and walked into the dining area. Henry looked around. Everything was so typical of a Chinese restaurant, with the gold and red calligraphy and caricatures of Oriental scenes. On the far wall he could see a large golden dragon, and facing it was a golden Phoenix. Red paper lanterns graced the ceiling, along with a few chandeliers. The girl stopped at an oak table with gold chairs, situated in a quiet area near the wall.

"Here you are," she said. Henry smiled and thanked her. He pulled out a chair and sat down across from a petite Asian woman, dressed in a conservative, royal blue suit with a white shirt. Her black hair was rolled into a bun at the base of her neck.

"Good afternoon, my name is Miss Yang. And you must be Henry," she said.

"Nice to meet you," he said and offered his hand. They shook hands. She had a cup of Chinese tea in front of her. Her delicate hand reached over to the teapot and poured him a cup.

"Tea?" she asked and slid the cup toward him.

"Thank you. I won't take much of your time. I need to know if you could identify this woman, and tell me where to find her and who might have hired her?" Henry asked. He placed his hand in his pocket to retrieve the picture of the girl from the inn. He passed it to her. She examined the photo for a minute, and then gave it back to him. She nodded to him.

"Yes, I know her. Her street name is Gigi. She used to work at one of the parlors on Essex Street, but got fired a few weeks ago. A woman named Ruby Stone called me from New York and asked me to find her a girl. Why do you want to find her? Please, be straight with me if you want to know where to find her," she told him and took a sip of tea. She never took her eyes off Henry, which told him not to try to deceive her; otherwise he wouldn't get any information.

"My employer is an affluent person who was drugged by this woman named Ruby, who we think was hired by his brother. She stripped him naked. I believe she recruited this woman you called Gigi. She was part of the plan to destroy my employer's relationship with his girlfriend, whom his brother doesn't approve of. That's why I need to talk to her. I suspect they took photographs of him with this woman in compromising positions and they sent them to his girlfriend. One more thing, would you know how I could contact Ruby?" he asked very seriously. He picked up his cup of tea and started to taste it, but put it down and added, "Just to let you know, if I ever hear any of this conversation being repeated I might get upset, do you understand?" He didn't move with his hands folded on top of the table. She stared at him and it seemed that she was evaluating the situation. She nodded once at him then smiled.

"Your secret is safe with me," she answered and continued to sip her tea. Henry figured she was waiting for payment before she said anything further about this girl.

"Let me pay for our tea, it's on me." He took out his roll of bills from his pocket and concealed it under the table. He counted out twenty of the hundred dollar bills, then folded them. He put the rest of his wad of bills back in his pocket. He took the money in his hand and positioned it under the teapot. She didn't budge except for her eyes, which she cast downwards for a few seconds to assess the payment. She was evaluating the amount of bills under the pot and the information he had asked for.

She took her tiny manicured hand and discreetly pushed her clutch bag next to the pot where the money was resting, opened her small handbag, and smoothly slipped the bills inside it. She then took a pen and a piece of paper out of her purse. He watched as she wrote down an address and a New York phone number. She passed the note to him. She stood up and without another word, she nodded and walked out of the restaurant.

***

Logan was lying down on his back with his hands tucked under his head, wide awake. He glanced at the alarm clock and read nine o'clock. He felt the boat's slight rocking, even though it was docked. *It must be windy.* He turned his head and looked out the window. The weather looked gloomy. Dark clouds covered the sky. It would probably rain, or maybe it was just that he was in a somber mood. He had gone to bed the previous night wondering if Henry would be able to find the people responsible for this incident. Henry still hadn't returned by three o'clock and he must have fallen asleep. He didn't feel like getting out of bed or even taking a shower. He was disheartened by the whole situation. Embarrassed, too! The only thing he had on his mind was Bailey. *How am I going to get her back? It definitely won't be by staying in bed.* He turned his head to look at the empty pillow beside him. He grabbed the cushion and brought it to his face. He inhaled deeply, hoping to get a hint of Bailey's scent, her lovely fragrance he missed so much. He squeezed the pillow against his chest. He didn't know what to do.

He decided to check and see if Henry had returned from his outing. He picked up his phone and dialed Henry's number. *No answer. Now what? Where could he be?* He had to be patient, because he knew Henry sometimes disappeared for days on end when he was gathering facts for him. He would eventually come back.

He lay in his bed pondering why Bailey was so upset. He couldn't understand what he could have done, unless it stemmed from what had happened at the inn. Whatever it was, he would make it right.

He would send her flowers again, tell her he loved her, and ask to see her. Then he could ask for forgiveness for whatever she thought he did. He couldn't live without her. He would do this every day until she spoke to him. He was not going to give up so easily. He adored her. She was his soul mate; he was sure of it.

He buzzed one of the stewards to find him a florist in Boston and order three dozen red roses. He wanted them delivered immediately, to the vet's clinic. He sat on the edge of his bed, puzzled by why Henry had not come back to the boat last night. *I hope he's okay!* He always worried about his friend, but Henry was a big boy, he could take care of himself. Henry was Logan's only true friend. He didn't know what he would do if Henry had been hurt or something worse happened to him. He shook his head. *No, no, don't even think that way. He is just fine.*

He got up, dragging his feet as he walked to the bathroom. He looked at himself in the mirror. He leaned forward and put his palms down against the countertop. Logan shuddered, horrified by what he saw. He looked a mess. He hadn't shaved in days; his whiskers were long, and his hair was greasy. It was too long, hitting past his shoulders. He desperately needed a haircut, and he had circles under his eyes from lack of sleep.

He decided to rectify the problem. He couldn't live without her. *This was insane! How could I love so profoundly in such little time?!* He had to go see if she would talk to him. He picked up a razor and shaved his whiskers away. He figured a shower might make him feel better. The hot water washed his troubles away momentarily, and invigorated him back to life. He decided he would check to see if Henry was back as soon as he got dressed. Logan dried off, slicked his hair back and put on a pair

144

of True Religion jeans and a white T-shirt, then he slipped on a pair of black Fry boots.

He went down the stairs to the main deck to look for Henry. He asked the crew if anyone had seen him or heard from him, but no one had spotted him since yesterday.

Logan decided to drive to the clinic to see if perhaps Bailey might be in a better mood, hoping they could talk. He told a steward to have Henry call him on his cellphone when he arrived back on deck. Logan grabbed his helmet and took off on his motorcycle toward Newton, committed to finding Bailey.

CHAPTER 15

It was mid-morning and Bailey was working at the front desk, confirming the next day's appointments, when a flower delivery man appeared at the front door. She hung up from her last call and glanced up to see him holding an extremely large bouquet of red roses. She stood up to greet him and watched as he approached the reception area.

"Good morning. I'm looking for a Bailey Winters?" the man asked her as he placed the flowers on the counter near her.

"I'm Bailey," she answered, not thinking the flowers belonged to her.

"These are for you. Have a great day." He turned around and headed out the front door without another word. She leaned forward and smelled the aroma of the roses. *Who would be sending me flowers?* She pivoted the vase to find the card that was attached to one of the stems. She opened the small envelope and read the card.

"I love you, see you soon, Logan." A rush of anger came upon her. *How dare he send me roses after what he did?* She crumpled the message in her hand and threw it in the wastebasket next to her desk. She seized the whole bouquet of flowers in her hands and walked toward the kitchen lunchroom in the back. She opened the trash receptacle and threw them in it. She shoved them in forcefully with her hands until she couldn't even see the stems.

He has some nerve, to send me flowers after how he humiliated me. If he thinks I'm a fragile little China doll or his playmate, he's going to find out differently. I will not bow to him or take him back. She folded her arms in front of her and closed her eyes. She took a long breath and exhaled, hoping to erase the hurt she felt in her heart. She was reliving the horror of seeing those photographs. She sighed deeply again, trying to calm her nerves. She did love him, but she couldn't forgive him. She took a moment to compose herself, and held her head high as she walked back to the front desk. She didn't want her co-workers to see her mad, because then they would ask questions she was not prepared to answer or talk about. It was too painful. "Give it time. Time will heal your wounds," she told herself. She picked up her appointment book and lifted the phone receiver to continue confirming appointments.

Hours passed slowly as she tried to get back into her routine. She looked up at the clock and saw it was noon. She wasn't hungry, though. Logan was still in the back of her mind. At lunchtime she decided she would get some fresh air, and maybe when she came back she would feel better. There was a park two blocks away, where she could walk and clear her head. She advised her coworker that she was going out for a bit. She picked up her pocketbook and walked outside.

The light wind was warm, and Bailey could feel the rays of the sun on her face as she strolled down the street. It was a good idea to stretch her legs and try to erase him from her heart, but she couldn't forget the time they had spent in the islands.

She walked up the cobblestone pathway to the entrance of the park area as she noticed a motorcycle going down one of the streets that bordered the gardens. It instantly reminded her of Logan, and her heart swelled. She walked slowly and blindly toward the center of the garden. She saw an empty bench not too far away, so she headed toward it.

The park was a quiet place, with large oak trees and a pond with several geese. Children were throwing pieces of bread near them and observing them gobbling up the crusts. Within minutes she was at the bench. Bailey sat down, extended her legs, leaned her head back on the back of the bench, and closed her eyes. She could hear the birds chirping in the trees and some kids' voices while playing at the nearby at the recreation play area. She had been relaxing for about ten minutes, almost napping, when she heard someone say her name.

"Bailey," he said in a soft low voice almost in a whisper, but she heard it and recognized it on the spot. Her eyes flew open as she sat upright, her arms flailing outwards from the unexpected arrival. Logan was standing in front of her, his hands by his sides. In one hand he was holding his helmet. He looked so handsome, and his curls moved around with the wind. *Don't go there!* She narrowed her eyes at him.

"What do you want? Are you following me, now?" She glared at him without moving a muscle.

"I saw you when I passed by, riding down the street. I came to see if you were free for lunch. I was hoping we could to talk," he said, taking a step toward her. She stood up quickly when he approached her. She longed to touch him, but she couldn't. He'd hurt her too much. She couldn't go back to how it was before. No matter how much she wanted to hold him again, it was impossible.

"I have nothing to say to you. I don't want to be with you any longer. You need to leave me alone and move on with your life," she said sternly. Bailey tried to get past him to return to the office, but he was blocking her by standing in front of her.

"I love you! I don't know why you're pushing me away. Please, talk to me," he begged. She saw anguish written all over his face. She saw his right hand rise up as he went to touch her.

"Get out of my way. We are finished. I don't love you. Just leave me alone," she said, and tried once again to get past him. She clenched her jaw to keep the tears from building in her eyes. She told herself to run away, but her heart was telling her to embrace him. She just wanted to be held in his arms, to be kissed by him once again. She couldn't, because she would never be able to leave his side or trust him when he told her something. *He betrayed me!* It didn't matter what words he told her, deep down there was a knife he had plunged in her heart and the scar held by her heart would never mend.

She passed him and kept moving forward, one step at a time. She wanted to look back, but didn't. She felt the teardrops fall as she got to the edge of the entrance of the park when he yelled her way, "I love you and I'm not letting you go, do you hear me? I love you!" She didn't stop or acknowledge him. She just quickened her pace back to the office.

***

Logan had hoped when he saw Bailey enter the park that they could resolve their misunderstanding. He'd stopped about ten yards away from the bench. Without making any noise, he'd crept closer to her. He'd stood a foot away, just observing her for a minute with her eyes closed as the sun beamed off her hair, her delicate hands by her side, just relaxing. He'd missed looking at her beauty. He'd yearned to touch her, but he didn't what to scare her, so he'd admired her from afar.

Now he regretted the encounter. He stood alone with his helmet in his right hand, his eyes on her, watching her march away until he couldn't catch sight of her. He felt empty once again. She hadn't even turned when he told her he loved her. He was crushed. *What the hell has made her so cold toward me?* He bowed his head, his shoulders slumped forward, and his heart ached as he hauled his ass back to his bike. His eyes filled with tears, but he blinked them away. He would not give up on her that easily. He put his helmet on, lifted his leg and got on his Harley. He headed back to his yacht. He needed to find Henry; he could help him decipher what was going on. Maybe Henry had the answers to why Bailey kept pushing him away. *It has to have something to do with that woman from the inn.* As he drove back to his yacht, tears filled his eyes and he let out a loud cry of anguish.

***

Bailey's legs were exhausted before she reached her office building. She was almost there, but had to rest. Her whole body was shivering from seeing him again. She felt helpless. Her emotions were taking over, and she didn't know what to think. She loved him so much. How could he cause her so much pain? Not only did he hurt her by being with that woman, he tortured her with his gifts of flowers and showing up to see her. That was the worst. If Logan wasn't around, maybe she would be able to forget him.

She leaned against the outer wall of the building as her mind went back to the meeting in the park. Her mouth was parched from running; she needed something to drink. She slowly crept along the wall to the diner, three doors down. Her feet were heavy and the anguish she felt was deep. How was she going to escape this? As long as he was around, she would not be able to go forward in her life.

She pushed open the glass door of the diner and walked inside. She needed to sit down. Her head was spinning and she felt flushed. She noticed a few heads turned her way. She imagined everyone was watching her, but it probably wasn't so. She scanned the dining area quickly and saw a free booth in the back, by the window. She quickened her pace, hoping her legs would hold until she was seated. Finally she made it, and looked down to see her hands were still trembling. She hid them under the table. She surveyed the street to see if Logan might have shadowed her to the restaurant, but the coast looked clear. He was nowhere to be seen.

She exhaled heavily, trying to regain her composure. She had to talk to someone. *I'll tell Dakota. Maybe she will have advice, but I am not going to change my mind. Logan and I are finished.* The waitress came by promptly to take her order, but she wasn't hungry at all. Her stomach was in knots. She only ordered a tall lemonade. She dug her hand into her pocketbook and took out her cellphone. Bailey dialed her best friend's number. She couldn't deal with this alone; she needed a fresh opinion. She listened as it rang once, then twice. "Come on Dakota, answer!" she murmured.

"Hey! I thought you were dead. I haven't heard from you in a week. Funny how I was just thinking about you. How are you?" Dakota answered enthusiastically.

"Dakota, I really need to talk to you," she said in a shaky voice. She turned her body toward the window, so the other restaurant patrons wouldn't see how upset she was. She could feel her heart breaking, and she was trying to hold back her tears.

"Sure honey, what's the matter? Where are you? I'll come meet you," she said. Dakota was concerned by Bailey's tone.

"Thanks, I'm at the diner. You know, the small restaurant by my office. I'll explain everything when you get here, please hurry!" she told her.

Bailey was relieved Dakota was free and could come meet her. She opened her handbag and dropped her phone inside. Her attention was drawn to the yellow envelope that was protruding out of the inside pocket. A shiver passed through her. She touched it gently, almost afraid it might jump out. She pulled her hand back and closed her bag. She saw the server coming down the aisle with her drink. When the waitress placed it in from of her, Bailey looked up and gave her a slight smile.

"I'll just leave you a menu in case you decide to order any food, okay?" She set a menu down on the corner of the table and walked back toward the kitchen. Bailey reached over and sipped her drink. It soothed her dry throat. She kept squirming in her seat as the minutes ticked away while waiting for Dakota.

Her mind drifted back to the photos hidden in her purse. *Should I show them to Dakota, or just tell her?* She kept her eyes glued to the window, not wanting to look at anyone in the face. She lifted her wrist to look at her watch for the fourth time. *Where is she?* It had been twenty minutes since she'd called her friend. Finally she noticed Dakota's car coming down the avenue, and watched her park across the street in the shared parking area. She watched as Dakota exited her car, ran across the street, and entered the diner. She felt some relief when she saw her friend. She now needed to concentrate on how she was going to explain her situation with Logan to Dakota.

"Hi! What's the emergency? Why did I have to drop everything and get over here?" she asked, bending down to kiss Bailey on the cheek. Dakota slid into the booth with her. Bailey bowed her head as she held her hands around her glass. She couldn't stop her eyes from pooling with water. Dakota touched her hand tenderly and said, "Bailey, nothing can be that bad. So why don't you tell me what's going on, so I can help you figure this problem out?" Dakota whispered. She leaned forward and waited patiently until Bailey blinked her tears away. She nodded at her. Bailey lifted her head and looked her straight in the eyes.

"Okay. First, you know how much I love Logan. Well, he's here in Boston," she told Dakota. Bailey tried to keep her emotions in check so she wouldn't cry.

"That's fantastic!" She jumped in her seat. But Dakota's expression changed from happiness to concern when she saw tears falling from Bailey's eyes. Dakota's eyebrows squeezed together as she eyed her friend closely. She was confused.

"What's happened? I know you too well. Something took place. So spill it. Start from the beginning." Dakota grabbed a tissue from her bag and passed it to her. Bailey took it and blew her nose. She inhaled deeply and exhaled, nodding. Thankful Dakota was there to help her sort this mess out, she felt her shoulders untighten. She rolled them up and down.

"It all started a few days ago, when Logan's brother Riker came to see me. He offered me one hundred thousand dollars to stay away from Logan, but I refused." She was trying to keep her voice low so no one could overhear them. Dakota brought her palm to her chest as her mouth stayed opened. Bailey saw the waitress coming down the aisle once again.

"What can I get you?" she asked Dakota casually, as she stood by the table waiting.

"I really need a double vodka, but I'll settle for coffee right now," Dakota told her. The server smiled and went to retrieve her coffee. They sat in complete silence as Bailey debated if she should tell her the rest, but within a minute the server was back with the java. She set it in front of Dakota, then turned around and went back to her prep work.

"Okay, now tell me the rest," Dakota coached her as she poured cream into her coffee and picked up the spoon to stir it.

"Then the next day, Logan sent me a note asking me to meet him at Bar Boulud, at the Mandarin Hotel in Boston. I went and waited for him, but he never showed." Bailey bit her lip with uncertainty. She was not sure about proceeding with the event that happened that night. Bailey felt embarrassed, she could feel heat rising to her face. She avoided Dakota's eyes by looking out the window.

"Maybe he was detained or something happened, you don't know," Dakota tried to reassure her. Bailey shook her head.

"Bailey, what happened?" she asked with an uneasy look on her face. Dakota took Bailey's hand in hers and squeezed it. Bailey dipped her head toward her bag. She slowly stretched out her hand away and opened her handbag. She stared at the envelope, mulling over if she should show her friend the pictures. *What is she going to think?*

"Bailey what's wrong? Tell me!" She snatched the envelope out of the inside pocket and held it tight between her hands, still unsure. She reluctantly placed it on top of the table and slid it Dakota's way, but she didn't remove her hands from the top of it. Her hands started to tremble uncontrollably from nervousness. *What will she think of me, if she sees these photos?*

"First I want to explain to you that I do love this man. This guy came by the bar and delivered these to me. I didn't know this man, and I don't know what to think. I'm torn..." she whispered.

Dakota gradually pulled the envelope out from under her hand. Bailey didn't resist. She wanted someone else to see the photos and give her guidance. Dakota brought it close to her body, shielding it from the view of the other patrons. She leafed through them quickly. Dakota's eyes bulged out. From what Bailey observed, Dakota looked at most of them before she shut the envelope and placed it near Bailey's hand.

"Oh! My God! Who would...?" Dakota didn't finish her sentence. She put her hand in her jeans pocket, took out ten dollars, and placed it under her coffee cup. Bailey immediately retrieved the envelope from the top of the table and shoved it back in her purse. She didn't know what to say or do. She couldn't move, she was numb.

"Let's get out of here now, come on," Dakota told Bailey. Bailey didn't budge from her seat. She was like a statue. Dakota grabbed her arm and pulled her up. They rushed out of the restaurant as fast as their feet could walk. Dakota took Bailey by the hand and crossed the street. They went to her car in the parking lot.

Dakota opened the car door for her. "Get in." Bailey obeyed without saying a word, and sat down. By the time they were settled in the car, tears were falling down Bailey's cheeks. Dakota's hands rested on the steering wheel. Her eyes fixed straight ahead, and she was unable to speak. Not a word was said between them for the longest time.

"Now I understand why you're so upset. Do you think he sent them, or someone else?" she questioned. Bailey just shrugged her shoulders, still unable to speak as she sobbed.

Bailey sat motionless in the passenger seat of her friend's car. She was holding her handbag tightly on her lap. She was speechless. She turned her head to peek at Dakota, who had regained her color after the shock of the pictures.

"Let's think this over. First of all, I don't think he would have sent those photos to you. He wouldn't put himself in that position. He's here; I believe he loves you because he would not have come here if he didn't. Someone else sent these pictures. He came to find you. He followed you up from the islands to Boston, for God's sake! I repeat, someone else sent these pictures. Who would want to break you up? Think, Bailey!" Dakota was analyzing the situation. She looked Bailey straight in the eyes. She extended her hand and stroked Bailey's forearm gently. Her touch made Bailey appreciate their long friendship even more.

"I don't know. Do you think these photos are recent?" Bailey asked. Deep down inside, Bailey knew the answer to her question. There was a date printed in the lower part of the picture. It was the time period of the night she was supposed to meet Logan. She just didn't want to acknowledge the truth.

"Maybe the photos are older ones and the person who sent them somehow altered the date on them, but I know they are real. I don't know what to think anymore. He says he loves me, but why didn't he show up at Boulud the other night? He sends me an invitation, then he doesn't appear? Where was he?" Bailey was thinking out loud. She crossed her arms in front of her chest as she tapped her fingers against her arm. She shook her head, trying to understand the reason why someone would do such a thing.

Dakota glanced out the window, thinking. She was holding onto the bottom of the car's steering wheel tightly.

"I think you should confront him. Ask him outright about the photos. Show them to him. Have you talked to him since he arrived?" she asked, still concerned.

"I've seen him. He even sent me roses at the office, but I sent him away. I was so upset I didn't want to talk to him; maybe I should have asked him. I would have answers," Bailey said, wondering why she hadn't been brave enough to stand up to him and challenge him to get those answers.

"Bailey I'm going to tell you what I would do, okay?" Dakota extended her arm and took her hand in hers. Bailey just nodded, listening attentively as she moved her body slightly toward her friend.

"I would face him and ask him about them," Dakota suggested softly. She raised her arms and embraced Bailey tightly.

"I know I should, and I'll think about doing that. Thank you for being such a marvelous girlfriend. I knew you would help me resolve this problem, and at least now I have options. I love you," Bailey said and kissed Dakota on the cheek.

"See you later. Keep in touch," Dakota told her. Bailey stepped out of the vehicle to return to work.

CHAPTER 16

Henry shifted his weight from one foot to the other, standing in the alcove of the building across the street from Gigi's apartment. He checked his watch; it was three o'clock in the morning. This girl better show up soon. Henry had been waiting for her since midnight. He leaned against the frame of the entryway. He saw headlights approaching down the road. A white car was coming down the street, and it stopped in front of her building. A woman in a short pink skirt, tight tank top, in stiletto heels exited the car and made her way to the front door. It was her!

He watched as she held on to the railing, going up the steps of the apartment building. She was probably drunk or stoned. The car drove away. Henry came out of his hiding spot and crossed the street, followed her down the corridor of her building, and within three strides he was standing beside her. She pressed the button of the elevator impatiently. She cast her eyes upon him, but didn't say anything. She placed her hand in her pocket and removed her keys. The doors opened and they both stepped inside. She leaned forward to push floor number three with her long, chipped red fingernail. The door closed, and Henry stood silently next to her. *That girl really needs a makeover.* He noticed her pink lipstick was smeared, her hair had several shades of brassy blonde, and her dark eyeliner made her look like a raccoon.

"What number?" she asked, keeping her eyes on him. She bit her ragged cuticles off her thumb, then fluffed her hair. She grinned his way. It made him want to vomit, just thinking about what she was after.

"Same," Henry answered without moving. He continued to watch her in the mirrored panel doors of the lift. She kept her eyes on him. The doors opened, and he accompanied her, a few footsteps behind as she walked to her apartment. She took her key out as she approached her residence. She inserted it into the lock and turned it. The door flew open and she entered unsteadily. Just as she was about to close the door behind her, Henry's hand stopped it.

"Hey, what are you doing?" she asked, holding on to the doorknob.

"Gigi, I just want to talk to you," Henry said.

She looked him over from head to toe, then gave him a sensuous smile that made Henry's stomach turn upside down.

"Are you sure you only want to talk?" she asked him, but didn't wait for an answer. She walked inside and down the hall to her living room. She sat down on her sofa, crossed her legs and placed her arm on the back of the couch. Henry followed. He stood in the archway and looked down at her.

"I just need information, and I will pay you generously for your time," Henry informed her. He leaned his back against the wall and watched her face light up.

"Really! How much are you talking about?" she asked, intrigued that money was offered.

"Depends on the info. First, I know you were at the Harbor Sun Inn last night. I want to know who hired you, and what went on in the bedroom with the guy. Don't even think of lying, I saw a picture of you," he stated, frowning at her. His eyes fixed on her. He didn't have time for any bullshit.

"Listen, I'm no snitch, but for the right price I might be persuaded to tell you a story," she answered. She licked her lips and smiled again.

"All right," Henry said. He stood up straight, shove his hand into his pocket and took out one thousand dollars. He kept the money in his hand and moved it from left to right in front of her face.

"Is one thousand enough? It's yours, if you tell me now." He was hoping she'd take the money.

"Okay, can I have the money first?" she asked as she eyeballed the cash.

"No, start talking," Henry hissed at her.

"Well, a lady named Ruby called me earlier in the afternoon. She never gave me her last name, and hired me for my services. You know what I mean, right?" she asked, and chuckled. Henry didn't react to her and scowled at her. He placed his hands on his hips as she continued.

"Okay, we met at the inn in the late afternoon, around five o'clock, and she told me to wait in the bedroom she'd rented until she came back. I did. A couple of hours later I heard a knock on the door, so I opened it. She was holding up a man by his waist. Handsome too! He seemed drunk. He could barely walk or speak. So I helped her bring him into the room, and then we laid him on the bed. She told me to undress him, which I didn't mind one bit," she giggled.

Henry was disgusted, thinking she'd had her hands all over Logan. He swallowed hard as he narrowed his eyes at her.

"Hey! You want a drink?" she asked. Gigi pointed her dirty finger toward the fridge. She proceeded to get up from her seat, but Henry said in a harsh tone of voice, "Sit the fuck down and finish your story." She sat back down on the edge of the sofa cushion with a discontented look on her face, but she continued.

"You don't have to be so rude about it," she said, looking up at him.

"Well, let's see. After he was naked, she made me undress and lay with him in bed in different positions while she snapped pictures of us. I didn't even get to fuck him, too bad. He was out cold. I don't think he could have gotten it up, if you know what I mean," she said, with a suppressed laugh. Henry's face turned red from anger. He had to get out before he did something he would regret, like punching that whore in the face.

"And that's it. Then I left. Now, can I get paid?" She extended her hand toward the money. He threw the cash on the floor.

"You're a real piece of fucking shit, aren't you?" he told her. He turned on his heel and walked away. Henry couldn't get out of her place fast enough.

"Thanks for nothing," he heard her yell out. He opened the door and nearly ran out. Now he knew why Bailey didn't want to have anything to do with Logan. She had probably seen the photographs.

He marched out into the cool night, relieved to be out of there. He stood in the middle of the street, wanting to go back up and teach her a lesson she wouldn't soon forget, but what good would it give him? He needed to calm down, so he kept his pace steady until he could no longer see her apartment building. How could they do such an unscrupulous thing to Logan?

The next thing he needed to do was try to find Ruby Stone. He looked at his watch. It was three forty-five AM. He knew this woman was in New York, but where? He had to go there if he had any chance of finding her.

***

Henry sat in the first class section of an American Airlines non-stop flight to New York City. He had hurried to the airport as soon as he left Gigi's apartment and he was lucky to get the last seat available on the flight that left Logan International Airport at six AM. He looked out the small window to see the sun coming up on the horizon. Henry was exhausted, but he wouldn't be able to sleep until he'd found the culprit behind this unthinkable deed.

He closed his eyes and tried to rest during the hour-long flight, but he was so antsy that he was unsuccessful. He kept thinking he had to find Ruby to get answers. His only desire was to clear Logan's name, and hopefully restore his future with Bailey, which appeared doomed at the moment. Time was of the essence, if they were to be reunited. He replayed in his mind what Gigi told him. *How could they do such a dirty underhanded thing to Logan? Who had hired Ruby to do the deed?* His brain would not shut down with all the questions. They kept surfacing one after another, without any answers. An hour and a half later, the plane landed at JFK Airport.

Finally he walked out of the terminal and flagged down one of the famous yellow taxis of New York City. Henry slid inside, sat back and told the driver to take him to the corner of 42nd and 7th streets. Not another word was spoken until he was dropped off. He paid the man when he dropped him off by the curb and headed to the heart of Midtown Manhattan. He plodded up several blocks until he was on 44th street. His stomach was growling from hunger and he was developing a headache. He massaged his temples. He realized he had been so preoccupied with his detective work that he hadn't eaten since suppertime the previous night. He scanned the area down the street for a place to eat and noticed a large neon sign up above the doorway of a restaurant called John's Pizzeria. *That will do.* He strolled down to the entryway and pushed the door open, then walked to the middle of the room. The restaurant wasn't very busy; only a handful of people were in the dining area. He picked one of the wooden booths further down the aisle so he could have some privacy. He sat down and the server came by within minutes with water, ready to take his order. He ordered a cheese pizza with a cola to drink.

He took his phone and the piece of paper with the number Miss Yang had given him out of his pocket. He punched the number in and waited as it rang. On the third ring a woman answered. "Hello."

"Good morning, I would like to speak to Ruby," Henry asked politely.

"Speaking," she answered.

"My name is Henry. Miss Yang from Boston gave me your name and number. I would like to meet with you to employ your services," he said very seriously and waited. The line was silent for a few moments, without any response.

"Meet me in Central Park West, in one hour, have a seat in front of Tavern on the Green. There's a bench by the entrance," she replied without emotion and the line went dead.

Henry looked at his phone and placed it on the table as he waited for his food to arrive. His pizza arrived shortly. He devoured every slice, each one faster than the other. Twenty minutes later he paid his check and marched out of the restaurant. He raised his arm to flag the first available taxi. He hopped into the back seat, shut the door and told the driver to take him to the intersection of Central Park West at West 66th Street on the Upper Westside. The ride was short and the cabbie dropped him off in front of Columbus Circle. He walked the short distance to the Tavern on the Green keeping his eyes open to see if he would spot Ruby in the vicinity, but he never saw her. The old building was now a landmark restaurant that had changed hands many times over the years since it was first built in 1870, as a sheep hold. It became a restaurant as part of a 1934 renovation of the park by the New York City's Parks Commission.

Henry quickly spotted the wooden bench on the right side of the entrance and sat down. He scanned the area for Ruby once again without moving his head, but he had no description of her, except the photo from the inn. He waited patiently as he tapped his foot on the ground and watched the people walk by. Suddenly he noticed a tall woman with long black hair coming his way. She was dressed in black jeans with a short leather jacket. Her hands were tucked inside her pockets. Her stride was confident and she looked straight ahead. Henry could tell she was taking stock of her surroundings as she approached him.

Henry stood up straight, clasped his hands behind his back, and planted his feet when she was a few yards from him. She marched up to him, eyed him and ordered, "Let's walk." She didn't wait for a response from him and kept her stride as she continued down a path toward the park. Henry kept pace with her without a word. They strolled the narrow path until they arrived at a series of benches lined up under large oak trees down on West Drive. She sat down, her back not even touching the bench—as if she was ready to pounce should she have to. She didn't turn her head to look at him. She kept her eyes forward, so he did the same.

"How may I help you?" she asked him, with no emotion in her voice.

"I basically want information about a service you rendered, and I am willing to pay handsomely," he told her. He watched her expression, which showed nothing.

"Why should I help you?" she asked, not changing her tone or moving her posture.

"Because I will pay well, and because an injustice was done to a good man," he answered, staring at the side of her face.

"Really. Which one?" she questioned, without even a flinch of any muscle. She seemed completely uninterested.

"The job you did a few days ago, at the Harbor Sun Inn," he told her. This time she pushed her red lips forwards and seemed to be thinking about his reply. Henry decided to let her brood and remained quiet, hoping she did have a little bit of compassion in her bones.

"What do you want to know?" she asked.

"I want to know who hired you," he answered. He watched her once again muse over her reply as if she was deciding if she should tell him. Henry kept quiet and waited patiently. He knew if he didn't wait she might just walk away.

"Why?" she asked. She wanted to know before she would answer his question.

"Let's put it this way. Logan is an honest man, and doesn't deserve what happened to him. I think it was my employer's brother who hired you to destroy his love affair, but I have to be positive. Riker is a jealous and domineering man. I also need the pictures. I am willing to compensate you for your perfidious action," Henry informed her. He hoped she would be willing to divulge her client. He waited without another word; she was motionless. *Will she tell me?*

"I believe you are correct, and already have your answer. So be it. I don't need to be involved in your quest for the truth or quarrels between brothers. A courier will deliver the pictures to you, so I bid you good luck," she answered and rose from her seat. She never looked at him. She just walked away, striding down the pathway without another word.

Henry sighed as he watched her disappear into the crowd of passersby. She did have a conscience underneath that stony appearance. He sat in the park on the bench for a few minutes, kicking around if he should call Logan and explain what he had found, or have him come to New York to confront his brother. He really was concerned about what Logan might do when it was revealed Riker was the cause of his misfortunes.

He took out his phone and dialed Logan's number. It rang twice before he heard the familiar voice say, "Hello, Henry, where are you? I've been worried sick. Are you okay? What did you find out?" Logan's voice seemed agitated, but Henry didn't want to reply to his inquiries until they were face to face.

"Logan, listen to what I'm going to tell you very carefully. I want you to take the first flight out to New York. Don't ask me any questions now. I will answer all of them in due time, sir. I will meet you at your condominium," Henry told him.

Logan replied, "Okay, but..." Henry hung up the phone before he could finish his sentence.

***

Logan knew the minute Henry told him to come to New York he had found the guilty party. *Why didn't he want to talk to tell me on the phone? I just hope it isn't who I think it might be–Riker!* He threw his phone on the top of the bed covers and marched directly toward the closet. He swung the door open, took out his Louis Vuitton carry-on and placed it on the bed. He went to the dresser to pick up a couple of things, and started shoving a few essentials in the bag.

He reached to his back pocket and took out his wallet. He slipped out his credit card to call the concierge on his Black Centurion American Express for a reservation. He didn't want to fly commercial. He needed to get to New York as soon as possible. He looked down at Precious and petted her head as she slept quietly near him on the bed. He was taking Precious with him. Arrangements were made for a chartered flight on a Cessna Citation jet. Within an hour he sat in a leather chair on the private plane, headed for New York City's JFK Airport, with an approximate time of arrival in two hours.

Precious was by his side in her quilted carrier, her head sticking out on one side. She was sleeping soundly, and had ever since they had boarded the plane. Every time he looked at her it reminded him of Bailey. *How thoughtful she was that day, to buy him Precious. She knew I was alone most of the time, and she hit the nail on the head when she gave me this little bulldog. No one ever took the time to really understand me or knew what I might want. A perfect gift; something alive, like this puppy. Only her!* He loved Precious. He needed the puppy even more now than ever, because Bailey was not with him.

He turned away from Precious and stared out the small oval window as he flew over the clouds. *I have to reunite with Bailey. This cannot be the end.* He longed to have her by his side, whispering sweet nothings in his ears. He craved the touch of her velvety skin. He closed his eyes and tried to take a nap, but his thoughts would not let him sleep. He shifted in his seat, trying to get comfortable by adjusting his pillow. *Damn! I just can't sleep!* Finally, he gave up. Logan unbuckled his seatbelt and took three steps forward, toward the front cabin.

Up on the wall of the aircraft was a rack of different newspapers and magazines from around the globe, in several languages. He moved the magazines around and settled on the Sports Illustrated and Time magazines. He took them back to his seat, and sat down. He tried again to relax. He pushed the button of his seat back to recline it and started to read, but his mind drifted back to Bailey. *I hope Henry has all the answers. Henry must have discovered the facts otherwise why would he want me to travel to New York? I'll just have to be patient until I meet him at the condo.*

***

Henry arrived at the 22 Central Park South building within an hour of leaving the park. He entered the lobby area. The concierge and a security guard were sitting at a desk. They greeted him as he walked in. He waved at them, but he didn't stop to chat with them as he usually did when he came to Logan's residence. The building only held seven condominiums. It was a grand place, with marble floors and a huge chandelier hung in the middle of the entrance.

"Good afternoon, Henry. How are you?" the guard asked him. They were familiar with him coming and going from the home.

"Very well, Michael, thank you," Henry replied, and continued his stride. He walked directly past them to the elevator and pushed the button to the penthouse. He headed straight upstairs to Logan's condominium, which was located on the top floor. Many years ago Logan had given him a key.. Henry turned the key, pushed the door open, and walked in. He shut the alarm system off. His body was physically drained so he went directly to his bedroom at the end of the hall, near the kitchen. He immediately took his clothes off and threw them on the chair next to his bed. He entered his private bathroom and opened the shower faucets, then stepped into the shower under the hot water. He relaxed as the water ran down his body and took away some of his fatigue. Within ten minutes he had showered and dressed in a pair of clean trousers and a button-down shirt.

He went to his closet, reached up on the top shelf, and pulled a small black box down. He carried the box to the edge of his bed and laid it by his side. He punched the combination to open the secured container. Inside the locked box were a compact semi-automatic black Glock 21 and a ten round magazine. He took hold of the handgun in his right hand, then he picked up magazine with his left. He inserted it inside the grip of the gun and made sure the safety was on. He lifted his shirt and concealed the weapon in the waistband of his pants. He stood and put the empty box back to its original place.

He felt better so he decided to wait for Logan in the grand room. He stopped midway, in the kitchen, to open the refrigerator door and grab a bottle of Perrier. He strolled to the living room and sat down in one of the corner chairs facing the entrance, opposite the fireplace. From that location he would be able to observe the front door. He laid his head on the back of his chair, crossed his feet in front of him and closed his heavy lids. *How am I going to break the news to him that his brother was responsible for him losing Bailey?* That was all he could think about, but within five minutes, overtiredness took its toll and he drifted into sleep.

***

Bailey lay awake in her bed at the break of dawn. The sun was just starting to break over the horizon. She buried her face in her pillow, angry because all she had done was toss and turn all night. She couldn't have gotten more than three hours sleep. As soon as she would wake, Logan would haunt her. She was exhausted from the restless night. Her head was heavy and her neck hurt. She didn't want to get out of bed. She pulled the covers up to her shoulder as a chill passed down her back. She wished she could forget all her memories about Logan. *How could he deceive me like that?* She'd truly thought he was falling for her. *He's just like all the other men. They take and take, then dump you when they're done with you. Maybe Riker was right? All he's done is bring sorrow in my life since I returned home from my cruise. Someone had balls to send me pictures, to warn me against him. That was the last straw! I will never trust him again!* Her hands balled into fists as she thought about how he could be so underhanded—to invite her to the bar, then not show up.

Wait a minute! She sat upright in her bed. She grabbed the folder from her side table and emptied the contents on top of her bed covers. She picked up one of the photographs and examined it closely, then studied the next one, and so forth. She inspected every one of them carefully. In none of these pictures, not one of them, did Logan have his eyes open. None of the pictures portrayed him kissing or holding her. She seemed to be always on top of him or by his side, but he was never participating fully. *Strange! Why?* She laid her head against the headboard thinking. She looked at the photos scattered on the bedspread. As much as she hated to look at them, something was not right. But what? Suddenly it occurred to her. *Maybe it wasn't Logan who had sent them. Maybe he didn't know about them, and maybe, just maybe, it was someone else who sent them. But who? And how did he end up in bed with her?*

Son of a bitch! She picked up all the photographs and returned them to the envelope. Dakota was right. She would confront him, because maybe he really didn't know about them. Maybe they were old pictures from a time before she met him. *Why would he have tried to talk to me and come to see me, if he knew about the pictures? He even sent me roses. Someone set me up! Riker! Riker detested the way Logan was happy with me, and he has tried to keep me away by bribing me. I have to find Logan!*

She pushed the covers aside and jumped out of bed. She ran to the closet and took out a pair of jeans and a sweater. She dressed as fast as she could. *I have to find him,* she kept repeating in her mind. *He probably has his yacht. There can't be too many marinas that can accommodate and dock his ship.* She sprinted to the kitchen to find a phone directory that listed the marinas around Boston. She was determined to find him, if it was the last thing she did. Logan hadn't done anything wrong and she had pushed away her only chance at love. She opened the phonebook and leafed through it until she found the piers. She wrote down three public marinas. She picked up her handbag, car keys, and her note, then headed out the door. She had a good feeling. She just hoped Logan would forgive her for being so cold toward him.

She drove to the first place on her list, Constitution Marina, and parked her car in the parking lot. She got out of her car and walked to the gate, stopping at a security booth. She inquired if a boat named *The Vagabond* was docked at their marina. She watched as his finger went down the checklist of boats. The security guard told her there was no yacht by that name docked at this pier.

She returned to her car disappointed and drove to her next destination, Boston Waterboat Marina. As she approached the lot and parked her car, her heart jumped a beat because she could see *The Vagabond*. She hurried down to the pier and walked past several boats, paying no attention to the people passing by. Her eyes were glued to the last one at the end.

Bailey slowed her pace. She saw the name written on the yacht. She was right. She wasn't too late. Now if Logan would just see her. She stepped up the side boarding stairs one at a time. She held on to the railing tightly as she arrived at the top. A deckhand looked up at her as she boarded the ship. He seemed to remember her and greeted her.

"Good morning, Miss Winters. How may I help you?" he asked, as he took her hand in his to help her aboard. She stood still, feeling the boat sway slightly from side to side. She scanned the area behind him, but she didn't see Logan or Henry. It was early morning, so maybe they were inside sleeping.

"Hi, I'm looking for Logan. I would like to speak to him. Could you tell him I'm here please?" She asked and stepped to the sideway and went down to the outdoor bench.

"I'm sorry, Miss, but he isn't here," he replied.

She looked up at him, disappointed, and sat down on a lounger.

"I'll wait. Do you know when he'll return?"

"I don't know when he will return. I believe he flew to New York last night," he told her. Her hands came up to her mouth. *Oh! No. He went home and gave up on me. Now what am I going to do?*

"Is Henry here?" Bailey asked as she held her breath. The deckhand shook his head.

"He's not here either. I do believe they are together," he answered.

"Would you have his address in New York?" she asked him as her eyes pooled up with tears. *If I have to go to New York to find him, I will. I love him and nothing will stop me!*

"I will tell him that you dropped by if you wish, but I can't give you that information," he politely responded.

Bailey just nodded and whispered, "Yes, please tell him I need to talk to him. Thank you." She stood up; her legs felt weak. She reached over and held on to the railing, afraid she might faint.

"Are you all right, Miss Winters?" the deckhand asked as he approached her.

"Yes, I'll be fine," she whispered. She held the railing tighter and took another step forward to disembark from the ship.

She had lost her only love. He was now gone. She found some strength from within and silently went ashore. She would never see him again; never feel his warm kisses or his arms around her. How stupid she had been! He'd tried to talk to her, but she pushed him away. Each step she took seemed like a dead weight pulling her down as she plodded wearily, heartbroken, on her way toward her car to return home.

CHAPTER 17

The elevator door opened to Logan's condominium, which covered nearly the entire top floor. He walked the short distance to his front door and entered. When he stepped inside, Logan dropped his bag at the entrance. He saw Henry get up from his chair and come toward him. Logan noticed Henry looked tired; he had dark circles around his eyes. He'd bet Henry hadn't slept since he had left Logan's side.

"Good evening, Henry. How are you doing? You seem drained, worn out." Logan said. He approached and offered Henry his hand. Henry grasped it and shook it firmly.

"I'm a little tired, but I'll live. Don't worry about me," he answered, with a wide smile on his face.

"Now that I'm here, tell me what you found. I'm dying to know," Logan said. They walked back to the living room together and sat down in the chairs that were facing each other. Logan noticed that Henry gave him a slight involuntary grimace. Why? What has he discovered in the past couple of days?

"I think you better brace yourself, Logan, because what I'm about to tell you is not good. It's shocking, in a way," Henry said. He placed his arms on his knees, leaned forward, and picked up an envelope from the table near him. He held it between his fingers like it was something repulsive, and looked down at it.

"I'm going to summarize what I tracked down. I found out the name of the lady you met at the inn. Her name is Ruby Stone. She drugged you that evening, and took you to one of the bedrooms, where she had another girl waiting," Henry told him in a gentle, fatherly voice.

Logan was staring at him, unable to believe what he had just heard. *Drugged? I was drugged?* His palms began to sweat from nervousness; he rubbed them together. Henry stopped speaking to contemplate his next words carefully. "Continue," Logan said.

Henry swallowed hard. "Well, this other girl was just a hired hand. They undressed you, and Ruby took pictures of you and the whore in compromising positions. The photographs were then delivered to Bailey." Henry stopped talking and handed the envelope to Logan. Logan took it from him with a shaking hand and opened it. He pulled out a few photos and gasped loudly at what he saw. He could feel his head start to spin as rage invaded his body. His adrenaline spiked; his heartbeat raced.

Now he understood why Bailey wouldn't have anything to do with him. He couldn't blame her! He would have felt the same as she did if someone had given him that kind of pictures. He closed his eyes and sighed heavily. He stood up, dropping the envelope on the floor. The pictures scattered, but he didn't care. He stomped his feet on them and kicked them with all the force he had. He stomped his way over to the large windows on his right, overlooking the lights of the city. His clenched his hands tightly on his hips. After a few minutes, once he had calmed down a little, he finally turned around to face Henry.

"Who the fuck is responsible? Tell me! I know you found out who did this," he demanded, clamping his jaw tightly. He could barely breathe. He already knew the answer to his question, but he needed to hear it from Henry. Who else had the guts to hurt him where it would pain him the most? There was only one person: his twin brother. Henry bowed his head for a moment and slowly glanced up at him.

"Answer me!" Logan screamed, with his hands still balled into fists.

"It was Riker," Henry replied, eyeing Logan closely.

"Are you positive?" Logan asked, slightly more calmly. He was hoping that Henry was mistaken. Henry nodded affirmative. He knew deep down in his heart that only his brother would stoop so low to injure him so badly. Riker knew it could destroy the only thing Logan truly cared about and loved: Bailey. This time Riker had gone too far.

Logan marched in a straight line, like a soldier ready for war. His arms swung by his side, and his face was like stone; he forged toward the front door like someone on a mission. He scooped up his car keys from the bowl at the door in one fast motion. He swung the door open and headed to the elevator. By the time he pushed the lift button, Henry was standing by his side. There in a flash, Henry never hesitated to accompany him.

"I'm coming with you. Give me the keys, I'll drive," he ordered, and stretched out his hand for the keys. Logan placed them in his hand. They both stepped into the elevator and Henry punched the garage button. Within minutes Henry and Logan were sitting in a Range Rover, flying down 59th street to Trump International Tower, where Riker resided on the 37th floor. Henry pulled the vehicle into the valet area. Logan leaped out and started running up the stairs to the entrance of the building. He bypassed the concierge at front desk and went directly to the elevators, without being announced to his brother that he was on his way to see him. Henry trailed close behind. Not a word was spoken between the two men. Logan was breathing so hard he could barely think. He was so furious at Riker.

"Logan, you need to settle down before you face your brother," Henry said as the elevator counted away the floors. Logan didn't say a word.

"Logan, you cannot go in there with your emotions on your sleeve. He will defeat you. Think before you act. Now relax, and cool down," Henry continued to warn him.

"I'm going to kill that fucking bastard, that's what I'm going to do," Logan spit out. Silence invaded the small space.

"Sir, please think about what you're saying! I know he's evil, but he is your brother. Don't do anything you will regret later!" Henry told him quietly. Henry was trying to smooth the situation over, but Logan didn't care anymore. This time there was no forgiveness.

Henry stayed close to him, afraid Logan might do something he'd regret later. Henry had followed two feet behind Logan, and was ready for whatever he had to do to protect Logan. The elevator doors opened. Logan marched forward to the front door, formed a fist, and pounded several times loudly on the door. He screamed, "Riker! Open the fucking door! I want to talk to you!" A few seconds later, Riker swung the door open. He was dressed in a blue pair of casual pants, with the hem of his white shirt untucked, and he'd unbuttoned it at the neck.

The minute Logan saw his brother standing in the doorway, he lunged forward and gripped his shirt in his fists. He forcefully pushed him backward until Riker stumbled backward and hit the wall behind him.

"You fucking bastard! Why? Why did you do it?" Logan yelled at him.

Riker didn't answered. He just kept laughing out loud at Logan, as if this was just a game. He pushed Logan's hands away from his shirt.

"What are you talking about, dear little brother?" He replied mockingly, and walked away. Logan's anger showed. His face was red, lips pressed tightly together, eyes narrowed, and he kept opening and closing fists. Logan was so distraught.

Riker walked into his library, where books decorated two walls from top to bottom and an array of leather wing chairs surrounded a fireplace. A carved mahogany desk was on the opposite wall, and a bar stood next to it. Logan trailed closely behind him. Henry stopped next to Logan, on his right. Henry stood erect, feet apart with his hands clasped behind his back, observing what was unrolling before him. Riker went to the bar area and grabbed a crystal glass, then poured a double shot of Johnny Walker Blue Scotch whiskey into it and gulped it down. Logan edged close to Riker.

"Answer me you bastard! Why? Why do you have to ruin all that makes me happy?" Logan asked. Riker, unconcerned, just poured himself another drink.

He moved back away from Logan and sneered, "Because, little brother, I can. She wasn't right for you. You'll get over it. She was just another one of your playmates."

Henry observed all this as if it was in slow motion. Logan lifted his arm and with a swift blow, punched Riker in the jaw; a solid right hook. Riker stumbled backwards, his backside slamming into his desk. Henry could tell by his grimace he was stunned that Logan struck him. His arm flew upward and he lost his grip on his drink. It went flying and shattered on the ground. *Good hit, Logan.* Henry beamed broadly. Henry didn't move from his position. He just eyed both of them.

"Don't you dare call her that!" Logan yelled, then clenched his teeth. Henry noticed Logan's body was still wound up tight, and his hands were still balled in fists. Logan stood like an animal ready to pounce on his prey.

Riker was shaking his head to regain his composure, and rubbing his jaw.

"Are you out of your fucking mind? This woman is not worth it," he screamed. He glared at Logan as he moved his lower jaw from side to side.

"You had me drugged and humiliated me by taking pictures of me with some hooker! And then, you had the guts to have the photos delivered to Bailey. You are really despicable. You disgust me! I hate to think we're brothers." Logan stared at Riker.

"Remember we're identical, brother. I'm just not afraid to show my true colors. You're just putting up a façade! Oh, poor little rich boy!" Riker said, laughing and clapping his hands. He bowed at the waist toward Logan.

"I might resemble you, but we are not the same. You are immoral. You belittle people who are not your financial equal. I have principles, you don't," Logan threw at him, still not budging from his spot. Henry saw Logan had started to sweat; a droplet slid down his temple.

"Principles! You're fucking blind. Someone has to protect you. She doesn't love you. She's a slut after your money," Riker said.

That was all Logan needed to hear. He rushed forward onto Riker, punching him two more times as Riker's back was pinned on the side of the desk. Henry didn't move, letting Logan have a few more hits. Riker fought back by grabbing Logan's shirt and swinging his right hand into Logan's eye. Henry watched them intensely, but didn't deter Logan from his battle. He would not interfere unless Logan was in grave danger. A fight was a fight. Riker rolled away from underneath Logan's grip. He staggered to the side of the desk.

"Enough!" Riker yelled. He raised his hands and took two steps backwards. Logan regained control, but was still breathing heavily. He stepped away, but they were only a few feet apart; Logan was still ready to pounce like a cougar.

Riker's face was bloody from Logan's blows. His right eyelid had a cut and blood was seeping out down his cheek. He brought his hand up to his face and touched his brow. He looked at his fingers.

I hope it hurts, you bastard! Henry observed his every move closely. Logan was not going to let him win this time. Henry chuckled quietly. *I hope it hurts, you bastard!* He stood by the door of the library, ready to help Logan if he saw he couldn't handle the situation. But so far, so good.

"You cut me, all over this—bitch. You're crazy!" Riker said and wiped the blood from his hand onto his pants. Henry kept his eyes on Riker.

Henry could tell he was furious that his brother had been able to get a few right hooks on him. Henry observed Riker was inhaling and exhaling hard, and his hundred-dollar shirt was ruined by the bloodstains. His face was bruised from Logan's punches.

"You are dead to me. I never want to see or talk to you, ever again. I'm going to marry Bailey. I love her, and she loves me. I don't care if you approve or not. It's my life and I will do as I please. You don't control me," Logan hissed at him, turned and started to walk away.

Logan had only taken a few steps away when Henry noticed Riker's hand move to the left, searching for something on the desk. He saw Riker grab a metal letter opener. His face contorted with anger, Riker raised his arm. He had a white-knuckle grip on the weapon. Logan had his back to him; he was unaware of what was happening behind him. Henry straightened up and spread his feet. Riker made a sudden lunge forward. Riker was attacking Logan! Or worse, he wanted to kill Logan!

Within a split second, Henry yelled out Logan's name. Henry took a step forward and forcefully pushed Logan out of the path of Riker's assault. Henry swiftly fished out his concealed weapon. Without hesitation Henry aimed and squeezed the trigger in Riker's direction. Henry desperately wanted to stop him from harming Logan.

**

Logan, headed out of the library,, glanced up at Henry's face when heard his name yelled. Henry's expression had changed from casual observation to one of fright. In an instant, he saw Henry raise up his arm, and he felt Henry's strong hand forcefully push him. Logan wasn't expecting to be violently shoved, and he tripped over his feet. He lost his balance and fell to the floor next to one of the chairs. Logan's nose-dive came too swiftly to prepare for; as he was thrown to the floor,. and pain went through his body. He heard a loud bang. It was a gunshot!. He turned over quickly upon and sat up on the carpet. He was confused, and unsure of what had just happened. He was dazed. *Why was I shoved to the floor? What's was going on? What happened?* His eyes scanned the room quickly, but he was unable to comprehend what had just taken place.

Oh my God! Logan's eyes bulged out. He saw Riker, Logan was sitting on the floor about six feet from him. Logan was in a state of incredulity. Riker was leaning against his desk, just standing there, his white shirt stained with red. Logan whipped his head around to look at Henry, who was holding his gun in his right hand. Henry had shot Riker! Logan realized it was blood on Riker's shirt. Riker fell to the floor. His eyes were wide open, and he was pale and clutching his chest with one hand. Blood seeped through his fingers. Logan saw that Riker had a metal letter opener in his other hand.

Henry ran to Logan, but Logan quickly crawled on his hands and knees to Riker. "Riker," he shouted as he approached him. Logan extended his hand toward Riker to help him. As he reached out to him, Riker raised his arm in an undeniable effort to wound Logan, swinging the metal weapon at Logan. Logan pulled back, but it was too late. Riker's letter opener hit him with enough force to slice Logan's lower forearm. A sharp stinging sensation of pain went through his flesh, traveling up his arm. Logan pulled his arm back to his body and covered the cut with his other hand. Logan stared wide-eyed at his brother.

"What the fuck is your problem? I'm only trying to help you, and you do this!" Logan yelled.

Henry's powerful hand gripped Riker's wrist before he could try to strike again. He bent Riker's hand backward, and Riker immediately dropped his weapon. Logan heard his brother moan loudly from the torture. Logan's mind was in a state of confusion. *He tried to kill me! No, he wouldn't. But he did!* There was no denying it. He looked down at the gash, a long, deep slash on his arm. He put pressure on his wound.

"Are you okay, Logan?" Henry asked urgently. Henry pushed the metal object away from Riker.

"Yes. I'm fine, Henry. Call 911, and hurry," he instructed Henry. Logan slipped closer to his brother who was losing consciousness. His eyes kept fluttering and his face was twisted into a grimace. He was in pain, and barely holding on to life.

"Riker, please hold on. Everything is going to be okay, help is on the way," Logan said in a sympathetic tone. Riker just nodded slightly. Logan saw a tear fall from Riker's eye.

"I'm sorry, I didn't mean..." Riker managed to say. His broken breathing was struggling to keep life into his body. Logan's heart broke and tears filled his eyes. Logan knew then; Riker wasn't going to make it. Riker's breathing was becoming more and more shallow. Riker's hand that was clutching his chest fell to his side.

"I know, don't worry. Stay with me! You're my twin, and I'll always love you," Logan screamed. Logan put pressure on the wound to stop the bleeding, but it didn't seem to help.

"Henry, please find a towel or something," he yelled. The whole front of Logan's shirt was red with Riker's blood.

"I...be happy...I love...too," Riker tried to whisper. Logan put his head closer to his mouth as he continued to talk to his dying brother.

"Riker, don't you worry. Do you hear me? Be strong! I'm right here." Logan kept encouraging Riker. Henry handed Logan a small white towel, and he pressed it on the wound.

"Riker, they're coming. Don't you die on me! I need you, Riker," Logan sobbed. Logan watched Riker's eyes roll back in his head, and he heard Riker take his last breath.

"Riker, nooooo!" Logan cried, tears streaming down his cheeks. Logan took Riker by the shoulders and shook him hard while screaming his name, but he got no response. Riker's body went limp. Logan sat beside his brother immobile, in shock.

The EMTs arrived. They told Logan to move aside, but he couldn't. Henry walked over and gently lifted up Logan, placing his arms under Logan's armpits. Logan could barely stand, much less walk. Henry placed him in one of the chairs. *Riker's not dead! They're going to revive him. I can't live without him. I didn't mean what I said to him.* Logan kept repeating this in his mind, over and over as he watched the paramedics try to resuscitate Riker. Riker lay on his back; someone was on top of him giving him CPR. Another paramedic started an IV. They lifted Riker's body as another EMT slipped a board under him. One of the paramedics listened to his heart with a stethoscope, but couldn't hear a heartbeat. He placed his fingers on Riker's neck and tried to find a pulse. He pulled his hand away and shook his head at the other EMT who was working on Riker. They both leaned back, staying on their knees to pack up their gear. They stood up and approached Logan. One of them kneeled next to Logan's chair and touched him on the arm.

"I'm sorry, sir. There's nothing else we can do for him. Your arm's hurt? Let me take a look at it," he said softly, and pointed at it as he rolled up Logan's sleeve. He bandaged it with gaze and tape. Logan had no feelings right now. He was empty, numb. *How did it get this far?* He was alone now. He had no other family. He felt a hand on his shoulder and looked up. It was Henry.

"Logan, I'm so sorry. But there are two detectives here. They're in the living room, and they want to talk to us."

Logan just nodded and stood up. He turned toward his brother, Riker, and took one last look at his twin lying on the floor. Henry took Logan by the arm and escorted him to the living room area. He heard someone say, "Cordon off the crime scene. Call the CSI people, and the coroner."

What was happening? It's like a nightmare he couldn't wake up from. He sat down on one of the couches, still in shock. Logan wasn't comprehending much when someone started to talk to him.

"Mr. St. James, my name is detective Santos. I'm from the NYPD. I'm sorry for your loss, but I have a few questions for you and I need your account of what happened here. Would you mind coming down to the station? I'll have you transported by an officer," he said.

"Henry? Where's Henry?" Logan asked quietly. He tried to focus on what was going on. He needed his friend. *He saved me! He didn't hesitate, thankfully, otherwise I might not be alive.* He didn't see Henry anywhere.

"He has already been taken to the police station. You can see him later," he informed Logan. Logan signed heavily, realizing what had transpired. Riker was dead. Henry had saved him from his older brother's assault, and hopefully Henry would not go to prison. It was self-defense; Riker had tried to kill him.

"I would like to call my attorney, please," Logan told the detective right away. All he could think of now was that he had to help Henry.

"No problem. We'll let you do that as soon as you arrive at the precinct. Now, if you'll follow me." Santos stood beside him in a blue suit, with his tie slightly undone and his badge dangling from his neck. He was a man in his late thirties with a very short haircut. Santos was holding a folder and a notebook, and waited for Logan. Logan nodded, stood up and slowly trailed behind him out of the condominium, on his way to the police station.

CHAPTER 18

When Bailey arrived back home, she stretched out on her couch and let the tears roll down her cheeks. She sobbed uncontrollably for an hour. What had she done? She should have talked to him when he came to her. She had lost him. She felt her whole world disintegrating in front of her, and there wasn't a thing she could do to stop it. He might never return to Boston, and she didn't even know how to reach him in New York.

She finally sat up and wiped her tears away with her hands. *What can I do to try to find him?* She slowly walked to her bathroom. She stood in front of the mirror, broken. *No! You will survive this, just find the answers. You are a strong woman, and you can do it.* She turned the cold faucet on and splashed water on her face. It felt good, and revitalized her. She picked up the towel and patted her face dry.

She decided at that moment she would return to the pier every day to check if Logan was back. She would ask repeatedly until one of his crewmembers gave her information about where she could find Logan, or at least a phone number where she could reach out to him. She was not going to give up so easily. She had more determination and strength than ever, to never concede defeat.

The first thing she thought to do was call her boss. She picked up the phone and dialed his number. She informed him she needed to take a few personal days off. She explained that she had a personal conflict she couldn't talk about, and she needed time to resolve it. He tried to talk her out of it, but reluctantly agreed to give her the rest of the week off, in the end. She hung up the phone and closed her eyes so she could think what her first move should be. She stood up, slowly walked to her kitchen, and opened the refrigerator door to grab a bottle of water. She picked up her handbag, which was on top of the kitchen island, and swung it over her shoulder. She also snatched a granola bar and an apple from a bowl on the counter. She bit into the fruit and chewed, then tucked the water and the bar into her purse. Now she was ready for a long day of surveillance. She marched out the door, on her way back to the dock.

Bailey was back at the pier within half and hour. She stepped out of her car and locked it, looking around at her surroundings. Bailey wanted to see which vantage point would give her the clearest view of the yacht, so she could watch it closely. She noticed a bench not far away, on the side of the dock by one of the stores. She headed that way while holding tight to her handbag. She sat down, laid her purse next to her and made herself comfortable. She glanced at her watch. It was only eleven in the morning. It was going to be a long day, but she was committed to waiting it out. She saw the deckhands cleaning the deck, and supplies being loaded on board. Hours went by without any signs of her love; it didn't matter, she was here to stay. He had to come back eventually.

Hours passed by and Bailey hadn't budged much from her spot. She watched the boats come to and leave the pier. People laughed, talked, and strolled down on the pier, eating ice cream or just holding hands. She only got up once, going to the nearest takeout counter to pick up a sandwich and something to drink. She looked down at her watch. It was now almost five o'clock in the afternoon. She lifted her head and examined the activities on the yacht.

There seemed to be something going on; The Vagabond was suddenly very busy. The crew was running in and out. The captain was on the deck, and one of the deckhands was unhooking the line from the pier. *Oh! No, they are leaving.* She ran down the walkway toward the ship. As soon as she arrived, she went directly to one of the few crewmembers who was still on the dock.

"Wait a minute! Are you leaving? Where are you going?" she yelled to him. He turned and looked at her, uncertain if he should say anything.

"Please tell me! Where are you going? Is Logan back?" she asked. Maybe she had missed him and he somehow got on board without her knowledge.

"I'm sorry, Miss. Winters. All I know is that we have a new destination. We are departing." He told her, and turned back to his work of untying the ropes.

"Wait, please! Is Logan back? Where are you going?" she hysterically asked. She reached out and touched his arm.

"Mr. St. James is not onboard. We are set for New York," he replied. He turned and left her standing in the middle of the dock as she stared at him, climbing on board the yacht.

"Wait, just tell me where I can find him!" She pleaded, but he paid her no heed and disappeared inside the ship. She heard the roar of the engines and watched in disbelief as The Vagabond pulled away from the pier. All her hopes of being with the man she loved were ruined. She was devastated. She bowed her head and tears appeared in her eyes. She let out a wail of anguish as she walked back to her car, unable to contain her emotions anymore. Everything was lost. She had been a fool! She had sent him away.

With trembling hands, Bailey took her car keys from her bag and unlocked the car door. She sat behind the wheel and dropped her head into her hands. She bawled her eyes out, for what seemed like an eternity. She was unable to stop the shaking of her body. She wept until there were no more tears. Her sorrow felt like a knife had been shoved into her heart. Her grief was enormous. What now? How could she return to her life? It wasn't meant to be.

She could try to find him, but New York was such a large city. She was overwhelmed. She had no way of contacting him. *I can't give up. I will never find another love like Logan.* She found a tissue in her bag and blew her nose. She started her vehicle, placed it in drive, and rolled out of the parking lot. Bailey tried to focus as she drove home in total silence. All that could be heard as she drove back to her apartment were the muffled sounds of a desolate woman trying to cope with the emptiness in her heart.

CHAPTER 19

Logan was first escorted to the emergency room by one of the officers. The doctor on duty sutured his arm. He received over twenty stitches on his forearm, but he was fine. They had given him something for the physical pain, but the torments he felt in his heart were beyond description. Riker was dead, and now Logan was worried out of his mind about what might happen to Henry. Henry had only protected him and he held no remorse against him. It was now Logan's turn to keep Henry safe, and out of jail.

Logan was soon sitting in a metal chair at a table in an interview room in the NYPD precinct where Santos worked in. He lifted his head and looked at the two-way mirror on the opposite wall, wondering if they were watching him. He had called one of the company's corporate attorneys, Richard Taylor. The attorney was on his way to the police station. Logan had briefly explained what had happened at Riker's apartment. Richard told him not to answer any questions whatsoever until he arrived. Mr. Taylor basically advised him to keep his mouth shut.

Logan heard a knock at the door and it swung open. Detective Santos and his attorney walked in. They both sat down. Richard took a seat next to him and smiled. He patted his arm and said, "I'm sorry for your lost. How are you doing, Logan?" He took out a pen and pad of paper from his briefcase.

"I suppose I'm fine," Logan answered. He felt so drained! Yet he still had to go through an interrogation before he could leave. *What about Henry?*

"We just need to know what happened at your brother's home this evening, so if you could start from the beginning..." Santos instructed. Richard nodded an affirmative toward Logan.

"Well, it all started last week, when Riker hired someone to drug me. He was trying to break up my relationship with Bailey, my girl-friend, who he didn't think was suitable for me." He stopped talking as his thoughts drifted to Bailey. How he wished he could hold her again, and that this mess was all behind him.

"Who did he hire, and what happened?" Santos asked, ready to take notes.

"Henry found out the name of the woman he employed was Ruby Stone, a private contractor for hire. She drugged my drink. She had inappropriate pictures of me delivered to Bailey to try and break us up. But it wasn't Henry's fault, what happened tonight. I came to New York to confront him, and we got into a physical brawl. I was on my way out the door, with my back to Riker, when I felt Henry push me. He shoved me because Riker was charging at me. He was going to stab me with a letter opener, so Henry protected me by shooting him." Logan hoped Henry wouldn't be charged with anything. Henry was just trying to keep him safe. Logan watched as Santos took notes.

They had gone over the story several times, and it was now past midnight.

"It's an ongoing investigation, but I don't believe you will be charged with anything unlawful. I do need some more specific informa-tion so I can check out the details. Your bodyguard will be detained for a few more hours," Santos told Logan and looked at his watch. Santos explained it was probably going to take a few days, and told Logan not to leave the country. Finally Richard and Logan walked out of the precinct and stood on the steps of the building. Darkness was upon them.

Logan could see the news media being held back by a police barrier at the other side of the street. He turned his back to them, then touched his attorney's arm and said, "I would like you to make sure nothing happens to Henry. He only tried to protect me. He didn't mean to shoot Riker and k..." he couldn't finish his sentence. The reality that his twin brother was dead was weighing heavily on him.

"I understand. From what the evidence shows, I don't believe they will charge him. It was just an unfortunate accident. I want you to go home and rest, for the moment. You'll have a lot to take care of, even without worrying about Henry. Leave that part to me," Richard said and patted him on the back. Logan just nodded at him and continued down the steps. When they reached the bottom, Richard raised his arm and flagged the driver who was waiting to take Logan home.

"Just go home. I'll go back inside, and check to see how it's going. I'll call you when I'm done." Richard opened the car's door for Logan and motioned for him to get inside.

"Thanks a lot, Richard," was all Logan could utter. He slid into the backseat, mentally drained from the day's events.

"I'll be in touch soon." He closed the door. Logan told the driver his address and he was on his way home.

CHAPTER 20

Bailey took a long, hot bath when she got home to try to ease and forget the pain she felt, but she still had a huge lump in her throat. She soaked in her tub for almost two hours, with her head resting against the back ledge of the bathtub. She finally decided she would have to move on with her life, as agonizing as it might be. Time would heal all her wounds. One day, God willing, she might see Logan again. She couldn't go chasing him all around New York City. She didn't have a home or work address, not even a phone number.

How stupid she had been when she left the yacht? She didn't think it would ever end. She pulled herself out of the tub, grabbed a towel from the nearby rack, dried off, and threw on a robe. She didn't feel like getting dressed just yet. She moped around the house, doing nothing. She went from room to room without any purpose. She made a cup of chamomile tea and brought it to her living room.

It was late, and she was sitting on the sofa swaddled up in a blanket. Her arms were wrapped tightly around her knees as she stared at CNN news on her television. Only the TV's light and a hallway nightlight illuminated the apartment. She preferred the darkness. She had no appetite. She sipped on her cup of tea, reminiscing about the time she had spent with Logan. Tears welled up unexpectedly, again and again.

She felt sorry for herself. *At least I have a few days off from work to get back on my feet.*

Her daydreams were interrupted when she heard a name she recognized, Riker St James. His name was mentioned on the breaking news. She whipped her head around and sat up straight. She searched around the cushions to locate the TV remote so she could increase the volume. She stared at the tube in astonishment as she listened to the anchorman.

"Breaking news—hotelier and business man Riker St. James was gunned down in his New York apartment this afternoon by the bodyguard of his twin brother, Logan St. James. In a report issued from the NYPD, spokesman Dave Safir said that it is an active investigation, and that they would have further information tomorrow. The only thing he would say, at this time, was that they believed it be an unfortunate accident."

Bailey's hands covered her mouth in shock. Her eyes were absolutely riveted on the television. Goosebumps passed down her back. *Riker's dead! What happened?* She now knew what Logan was doing in New York. Sadness invaded her, not for Riker, but at the thought of Logan being alone. He needed her. After all, it was his twin brother. Even though they didn't get along, she knew deep down Logan loved his brother.

Her mind was a whirlwind of questions. *What happened? Was Logan hurt? Was it Henry who shot Riker? Did it have anything to do with me? Why would it have something to do with me?* She sat motionless, unable to move. She wanted to go to New York to find Logan, but she didn't know where to begin. She figured she would be able to find out about the funeral arrangements through the news, or by searching public information on the Internet.

She sat back in her seat and closed her eyes. There wasn't anything she could do right now. It was going to be waiting game. She would check the Internet in the morning for more information. She got up and slowly walked to her bedroom, dragging her blanket behind her. She pulled the covers back from the head of her bed and slipped under them. Her whole body was fatigued, and her neck and back ached. She rubbed her aching neck. She needed to sleep so she could clear her mind and calculate her next move. But all she could think of was that Logan needed her. She would definitely keep checking the obituaries on the net. *He was a prominent figure, and the press will be on top of it. It seems too good to be true, but I might be able to hold Logan in my arms again. Thanks to Riker's death, even though it's a dreadful thing to think, I might find Logan.*

CHAPTER 21

Logan was at his penthouse apartment at 22 Central Park South, alone. He had arrived home around one o'clock in the morning. His rumpled, bloody shirt, was still on his body. His hair was mussed, and his body bruised from the fight. He couldn't stand the strain any longer. He covered his face with his hands and let his tears flow freely. He slumped down on the couch.

It was in the earlier morning hours, and he hadn't been able to sleep much, even though his physician had stopped by his condominium and given him medication to sleep. His agony over losing Riker was torture. It was something he had never experienced, and he wished his ordeal was over. Also, he was distraught about what might happen to Henry.

He stood on the second floor of his residence in the living room, staring out the large floor to ceiling window overlooking Central Park. He was dressed only in a pair of sweat pants. He recalled how he had taken a shower as soon as he had arrived home and watched Riker's blood wash away from his body. He shuddered at the thought. He pushed the handle of the patio's sliding door and stepped out on the terrace. The breeze felt good on his face; it warmed him. He walked out to the edge of his balcony. He felt so lonesome, and wished Bailey was by his side. Part of him wanted to die so he could be with Riker, his twin brother. Even though it had been bad between the two them, Riker was his other half. He was desperate for companionship and someone to cradle him in their arms so he could grieve. He had received many calls from numerous acquaintances and business colleagues, but he had let his voice mail pick up their calls. He didn't want to talk to anyone.

As he looked out at the green landscape of Central Park, he heard a few sirens from afar and the indistinct muffled noise of the city.

He walked to the edge of the terrace, his shoulders weighing heavy. He held tightly to the railing and bowed his head. *My twin is dead. How did it get so awful so fast? I'm alone now. I'm by myself. Alone! Bailey won't have anything to do with me, after everything that had happened. I can't blame her, but I love her so much!*

His whole being craved her. He closed his eyes and could smell her scent. He imagined the feel of her silky hair between his fingers, and her passionate kisses showered upon him. He couldn't hold in his tears any longer. A howling lament escaped him, as he wept bitter tears uncontrollably. The tears were in part for the death of his brother, but most of all, they were for losing Bailey.

His legs failed him; Logan collapsed to his knees. He sat on the balcony floor, with his back against the railing. He wanted to die. His hands covered his wet face in despair, and he screamed. He struggled to regain control of his emotions. Hours passed before the tears stopped flowing. Logan just sat there, unable to move. He was so lonely. He didn't have any life left in him, only a fortune. Money couldn't fill the emptiness that went down into his soul. *What am I going to do?* He mused on his hopelessness.

"Logan." His name being called out startled him. He lifted his head to see who was talking to him. It was Henry! A glimmer of joy and hope came upon him.

"I'm so sorry," Henry said. Logan couldn't respond. Henry approached him with his arms wide open. He reached down and lifted

Logan to his feet. Henry embraced him tightly. Henry put his arm around Logan's waist and assisted him to his bedroom.

"I'm here, it's going to be all right. Come on, it's time to get some rest." Henry gently sat Logan on the edge of his bed. He pulled back the covers, laid him down, and covered Logan with the blankets. Logan never uttered a word. He let Henry take control. He trusted this man. Precious tried to jump up on the bed, but fell. Henry picked her up and laid her near Logan.

"Have you eaten today?" Henry asked Logan, softly. Logan replied with a shake of his head.

"I'm going to make you some soup," Henry said. Logan glanced up at him with apprehension.

"I won't leave. Just close your eyes and sleep," Henry said using a fatherly tone, just as a father would comfort his child. Logan didn't object, and didn't say a word. He did as he was told.

Logan woke up two hours later, rejuvenated. He still felt a void in the pit of his stomach, but he felt better. He opened his eyes and noticed Henry, sleeping on the sofa next to his bed to his left. Henry had kept watch over him all day. He was a good friend. Henry probably needed him as much as Logan needed Henry at this time. Henry might be facing a murder charge. Logan knew Henry had only ended his brother's life because Riker would have killed him otherwise. He didn't blame him. He pushed the covers off himself and grabbed the top one. He tiptoed to where Henry was sleeping and tenderly spread the blanket over him, then left the room with Precious following close behind.

Logan walked to the kitchen and looked at the clock hanging on the wall. It was eight in the morning. He took a bottle of water from the fridge and walked toward his office. He slumped in the chair at his desk. He knew he had an enormous amount of work to do.

First, he needed to call the private number of his attorney Richard, to find out where they stood with the investigation. Then he needed to prepare a press statement. And lastly, he needed to make arrangements for his brother's funeral.

"Good morning, Richard. I apologize for calling you so early, but as you well know, we have a lot to discuss," he said. Logan glanced over to the shelf filled with pictures of him and his brother when they were younger. He looked away before he lost control of his emotions.

"No problem, Logan. How can I be of service?" he replied.

"Well, I suppose we have to deal with the media first. Then I have to see when they will release Riker's body..." he paused as flashes of Riker when they were little boys assaulted him.

"Logan, let me take care of things. That's the least I can do for you and your brother. I'll release a statement later this morning, announcing Riker's tragic death. I'll check with the coroner to see when we can have access to his body, and I'll drop by the police station to talk to Detective Santos about any new progress he's made, whatever information he has available," he informed Logan.

"Thank you Richard, I'm kind of lost at the moment," he said. Logan was grateful he was taking over.

"It's understandable. I spoke to Santos last night and they told me Riker had a security video camera in his office. They reviewed the video. The events that transpired were recorded, so you and Henry probably won't be charged. They evaluated it last evening Santos told me they all agreed, it was going to be marked as a self-defense matter. No charges will be laid against Henry, but I'll know more this afternoon." Logan breathed a sigh of relief as he listened to the news.

"Now, concerning the funeral, have you thought about what you wanted to do?" Richard inquired.

"I would prefer a small private funeral, if it's possible. I'm not sure if it will be possible, though, since he knew such a large community of people. I would like him to be buried at the estate in the Hamptons, next to our grandmother. There's a church nearby. I would like the services held there," Logan said.

"I can have my staff help you with those wishes. I'll get back to you later in the day or tomorrow with an update," Richard answered.

"Thanks again. I'll wait for your call," Logan told him, and shut the phone off.

CHAPTER 22

Bailey sat on the edge of her chair for the second day, glued in front of her television. She had barely left the house in two days, trying to accumulate details about Riker's funeral. Her computer was on her lap. She typed away at the keys, searching the Internet for any piece of information. She only went out to the local convenience store to buy The Wall Street Journal and the New York Post. The newspapers were quickly tossed on the floor next to her without finding any information.

She gripped the remote in one hand, listening to CNN anchors talk about Riker, when they stated that a private ceremony was going to be held at Most Holy Trinity Catholic Church tomorrow morning, with the burial at the church cemetery in the family plot, in the small town of East Hamptons. She jumped out of her seat and ran to the drawer in the kitchen. She pulled out a pen and a piece of paper to write down the information. She smiled. She finally had a lead. "I need to find Logan!" she exclaimed. It was all she had on her mind.

She had less than a day to get organized to get there. She walked to her bedroom in haste and opened her closet door. She grabbed a duffle bag and threw it on the bed. She opened the dresser drawer and took out a few articles of clothing: undergarments, jeans, and a few shirts.

She packed them neatly in her bag. She picked up her toiletries from the top of her bureau and placed them all into the bag.

She went back to the closet and chose a conservative black dress and shoes, carefully packing them into a plastic dress bag. She rushed into the shower, washed her hair and quickly got dressed, yanking on a summery, yellow dress. She tied up her hair, then hurried to the kitchen where her laptop was situated. She Googled the address of the church in East Hampton, and found it was a little over a hundred and seventy miles away. It would take her from four to five hours driving time before she arrived at her destination.

She typed in bed and breakfast with the church's zip code to search the area, hoping she might be able to get a room close by. She was in luck. She selected the Mill House Inn, which was in the heart of the village, and they had one room available. She booked it immediately, punching in her credit card number. Bailey made a reservation for later this evening. She was all set to get on the road. It was more than she usually paid for a room, but she knew it was a wealthy area.

She gathered her bags and walked out the door, confident that she would be reunited with Logan, or at least be able to speak to him about their situation. She sat in her car, turned the key and headed toward 395 South, on her way to East Hampton. The hours flew by, and night was upon her when she arrived in the town. She easily found the bed and breakfast. It was situated on the town's Main Street. She pulled into the circular driveway of the inn. Stopping directly in front of the historic brick inn, Bailey took a minute to look at the large windows with white shutters and wrap-around veranda. The grounds were beautiful, with large oak trees. She picked up her garment bag and got out of the car. She opened the passenger door and grasped her duffle bag in the other hand.

Bailey went up the veranda steps and entered the foyer. She was greeted by a middle-aged gentleman at the entrance. He was standing behind the front desk.

"Good evening. How may I help you? Do you have a reservation?" he asked her with a smile.

"Yes, I have a reservation. The name is Bailey Winters," she answered, and dropped her bag on the floor near her feet. She fished her wallet out of her purse and handed him her credit card.

"Yes, here you are. One room, with a queen size bed," he said. He returned her credit card, and she replaced it in her wallet. Bailey swung the strap of her pocketbook over her shoulder; seconds later, they were going up the stairs to the second floor to her room. She thanked him for escorting her up to her room and carrying her bag. She flopped on the bed, face down in her pillow. She was tired from driving, but she had made it.

Tomorrow would be a big day for her. She had to find directions to the church and the cemetery, if she could get through all the reporters. She noticed several media trucks parked at other hotels. She got up and took a few steps to the window of her room, looking up toward the stars. "I'm here Logan, I'm here," she whispered out loud. She decided to go to bed right away, and wake up early before all the reporters lined the street. She had to find Logan.

***

Logan arrived early in the morning by limousine, from New York to his grandmother's estate. Henry was glued to Logan's side, taking care of him. Logan greatly appreciated his devotion, especially after all that had happened.

Logan sat outside on the deck, relaxing with a vodka and tonic, facing the ocean and admiring the sunset over the ocean at his grandmother's compound. It was a beautiful home, built in the seventies when she had been in the prime of her life. His grandmother loved to have family around, so she made specific additions to the home for entertaining, with a large stone fireplace near the back porch to roast marshmallows after a long day at the beach. A basketball court was constructed in the backyard for the twins. His memories came flooding back as he remembered the good times with his brother in their younger days. He took another sip of his drink. He'd spent the last few days making arrangements for the funeral and dealing with the police; worst of all, the media was everywhere. He sighed heavily. *One more day.*

He sat thinking how lucky he was that Henry had been there. Logan never would have been able to cope without his loving ways and comforting touch. His biggest obstacle was he couldn't get over the thought that Riker hated him so much he would to attempt to kill him. He guzzled the rest of his drink, trying to forget the memories of the last few days.

He and Henry had been cleared of all charges. Richard was dealing with the press, and hopefully he could keep the majority of them away from the church and cemetery tomorrow. His thoughts sailed back to Bailey. He really wished she was here. He missed her so much. He looked at his tumbler; it was empty. What he really wanted to do was drown his sorrows in a bottle of vodka, but he knew it wouldn't help when the sun rose in the morning. Holding his glass, he stood and walked back inside to get another vodka.

Henry was waiting for him in the kitchen. He cut a chicken sandwich in two then placed it on a plate.

"I prepared you a sandwich and a salad. You need to eat to keep up your strength, sir," Henry told him, and placed it in front of him.

Logan looked at the food. He wasn't hungry at all, but he didn't want to hurt Henry's feelings by refusing his meal.

"I'm not too hungry, but if you sit and have half with me I'll eat a bit," he told Henry. Logan sat down on a stool and divided his meal. He pushed half of the sandwich toward Henry who had taken his erect stance on the other side of the counter.

"Very well then, thank you." Henry took the sandwich in his hands, taking a bite of it.

"And another thing Henry, please stop calling me sir. You're my friend and my only family now, so just call me Logan, okay?" Logan asked, picking at his salad with his fork.

"Yes, sir, I mean Logan," Henry replied between bites.

"Henry, I never thanked you for saving my life the other day. I understand it must have been difficult, and I'm sorry I dragged you into my problems, so thanks," Logan said. He looked up and saw Henry close his eyes tightly, as if he was thinking deeply.

Henry opened his eyes and said in a sincere tone, "Logan, you are my family and I'm sorry how things turned out, but I would do anything to protect you. I am also very sorry it ended like it did," he paused for a second and continued, "I just hope that after the funeral you go find Bailey and you work out things. She loves you. It was a really wicked thing Riker did to you. You should call her. You need her right now. She could comfort you in these trying times," Henry said. As he took the last bite of his sandwich, he reached over to nudge Logan's phone toward him.

"I tried many times today, but she didn't answer. All I got was her answering machine, she's not home," Logan explained.

Henry said, "Keep trying." With four long strides, Henry disappeared into the other room. Logan just stared at the phone, thinking maybe he should try again. He picked up his phone. He held it as he debated if Henry was right. *I have nothing to loose, right?*

He punched in Bailey's number and listened as the phone rang and rang, but she didn't answer. Disappointed, he put the phone down on the counter. He would go find her after the funeral was over and things died down. He needed to rest, because he knew tomorrow was going to be a difficult day. He got up and walked upstairs to his bedroom, hoping the sandman would sprinkle sand in his eyes so he could sleep.

CHAPTER 23

Bailey had a good night's sleep, and the next morning she was ready to go find Logan. First, she needed to find out where the church was located in this town. She walked down the stairs of the inn around nine o'clock and stopped at the front desk. The older gentleman looked up from his books. "Good morning," he said.

"Good morning. I was wondering if you could direct me to the Most Holy Trinity Catholic Church, on Buell Street?" she asked politely. She was wearing her black dress, ready to attend the funeral. She looked at her watch and determined she still had plenty of time to find it.

"Oh! You're going to the St. James funeral. Such a tragedy! Nice fellows, those boys. There's a lot of media in town. The only people allowed into the church are family members and very close friends. Apparently they have a checklist at the door. It's right up the street. You would be better off to walk up Main, and make a left turn two blocks up. That's Buell Street. You can't miss the church," he said as he pointed down Main Street.

She thanked him and took his advice to walk. *I'm probably not on the list.* She headed out the door and strolled down Main Street. She observed many news vehicles, including CNN, NBC, CBS, and ABC. She cast her sight to the reporters standing on the sidewalk, giving out reports concerning the funeral, and noted the significant police presence. The local police were parked along the side of the road, directing traffic and managing the crowds.

As she advanced closer to the church, she could see barricades set up along the route and hundreds of people moving around in the vicinity. She forged ahead until she arrived at the church parking lot. The church was an older one, built in 1894. It was a white wooden structure, with a steeply-pitched gabled roof. It was roofed in weathered wood shingles, and had large arched windows. The grounds were green and surrounded with large oak trees. She felt apprehensive, and was hoping she would be allowed to go into the place of worship.

Suddenly an officer stopped her, putting his hand out at the walkway of the church. "Excuse me Miss, this is a private funeral ceremony. It is close to the general public. You will have to stay in this area," he instructed her. She noticed he was holding a clipboard with numerous names on it. It was probably the guest list.

"My name is Bailey Winters. I'm a good friend of Logan St. James," she answered with confidence, hoping he would let her through to the church.

"Could I have your name again?" he asked, and looked at the directory.

She watched as he searched for her name, but she knew it wasn't going to be there.

"I'm sorry Miss Winters, but you will have to stand past the barricades. You are not on the list," he informed her. He pointed to his right, where hundreds of other people were standing and waiting for a glimpse of the motorcade.

"Thank you," she answered, disappointed. She wouldn't be able to go in. She walked over to where everyone not allowed inside was standing and waiting. As she plodded to the back of the crowd, she felt disappointment. *What can I do?* She could barely see anything above the heads standing in front of her. Twenty minutes elapsed, as the crowd grew even larger. The bystanders around her began to stir. To her left, she could see the procession of motor vehicles, headed by police motorcycles and followed by a hearse carrying Riker's body.

The motorcade drove up to the entrance of the church. She lifted herself on her tippy toes, trying to get a better view. Bailey's vision was partially blocked by other people in front of her. She watched intently as the funeral director opened the door of the hearse and the pallbearers took out a mahogany casket. They carried the coffin up the pathway to the entrance of the church. She kept her eyes on the car behind the hearse, believing that Logan had to be inside it. There he was! She caught sight of him getting out of the black limousine; Henry was by his side. Her heart swelled with joy and sorrow when she saw him. He had cut off the curly locks she loved to rake her fingers through. He was dressed in a black suit, with a white shirt and a black tie. Bailey couldn't see his eyes; they were hidden behind a black pair of shades. His head was bowed low and his shoulders sloped forward as he walked up the steps to the church. He was probably extremely tired. She wished she could be by his side to hold him, and give him a few words of encouragement. She needed to try to let him know she was there. She needed to reach out to him.

"Logan! I'm here!" she screamed, over the noise around her. She watched as he stopped walking momentarily to turn his head and look in her direction, but Henry nudged him on the arm and led him inside. He vanished inside the church.

***

Logan sat in the front pew, with Henry by his side. He listened to the priest conducting the ceremony, but his mind wandered back to when he entered the church. *I could have sworn I heard Bailey's voice call out my name. I'm imagining things. I desire her so much, I'm hearing things.* He stirred in his seat, wondering if Henry had heard it. He looked briefly at the wooden coffin resting in front of him. Memories of Riker assaulted him from when they were younger and had no worries, only a bundle of fun. His eyes watered, but he wouldn't let the tears fall. He was stronger than that. He focused his attention back on the activities unfolding in front of him and the bouquets of flowers that decorated the altar.

An hour later the services ended. He stood and followed Riker's casket out of the church. He stood near the hearse with his eyes fixed on the coffin, watching as the pallbearers carefully loaded it to go to the cemetery for the burial ceremony. Logan felt Henry's hand on his arm, pulling him back to the car. He nodded, pivoted on his heel, and walked back to the limousine. Henry held the back passenger-side door open for him. He slid onto the seat, moving all the way over to the opposite window so Henry would have a place to sit beside him.

Logan scanned the faces in the crowd, still hoping he was right and had heard Bailey's voice out there. As the vehicle rolled out, he caught a glimpse of a petite woman standing among the crowd. Her back was turned to him. *Stop, you're imagining things! You're just wishing for her to be here.*

"Henry, when we were walking into the church, I thought I heard Bailey calling my name. Did you hear someone calling my name? Or was I just hearing things?" Logan asked. He stared out the window as they rode down the street to the cemetery.

"I know how much you want her near you, especially today, and I know that you miss her, but I think you're mistaken. I didn't hear anything. I'm sorry," Henry answered with a small smile.

"I suppose you're right. Well, when this is all over, I'm going to go find her and try to get her back," Logan told him. He turned his head away from Henry as the limo rolled to a stop. He could see a green tent with chairs lined up under it. A grave had been dug in the family's lot, next to his grandmother's resting place.

"Here we are. Let's get this over with. The sooner the better," Henry said. He got out of the vehicle and held the door for Logan. Logan just nodded at him, stepped out of the car, and slowly strolled to a seat near the burial site. His sunglasses covered his eyes, which were full of tears. People were flocking around Logan, sharing their condolences and giving him words of support and encouragement. He really wasn't registering much. He shook their hands and made small talk. He was in his own world as he sat quietly, his hands on his knees, his sight anywhere, but on the casket. He didn't respond much to anyone.

The whole ceremony was agonizing, especially at the end when his friends, on their way out, laid a red rose on top of Riker's casket. Logan's eyes burn. He couldn't hold his tears back behind his dark sunglasses any longer. He felt them run down his cheeks. Everyone departed except Henry, who remained standing next to him. Logan couldn't move and no longer wanted to talk or see anyone. He felt so much remorse about the events that had led him here.

Someone was squeezing his left shoulder. He looked up and saw Henry. He hadn't noticed his surroundings for a while. He and Henry were the only ones left at the site other than the funeral director and the gravediggers.

"Can you give me a few more minutes by myself before we leave?" he softly asked Henry.

"Sure, no problem. I'll wait for you in the limo. Take your time, there's no rush," Henry answered. He trudged back to the car, parked not far up the road.

Logan sat in his chair feeling defeated. *How am I going to go on with my life, with Riker gone?* Even though they had been estranged the last couple of years, Logan knew Riker had always wanted what was best for him, in his own way.

***

Bailey waited patiently for people to leave, hoping for a chance to go see Logan. She didn't want to interrupt him while the services were being held. She stood behind a large oak tree, about twenty yards away. Her hands were shaking a bit. She was unsure how the meeting was going to proceed. She was afraid he would rebuff her, because she had pushed him away so many times. Her thoughts wandered back to their first date, when she'd had dinner with him and how gallant he had been in the restaurant. She brushed her fingers across her lips as she closed her eyes and remembered how his first kiss had pleasantly touched her lips.

She refocused her energy back to the situation. She observed as the last friend dropped a flower on Riker's casket and left the area. Logan seemed so sad, just sitting there with his head bowed. Henry spoke to him and left him sitting alone. She wanted to run up to him to comfort him, hold him tight in her arms, and whisper that it was going to be all right. She took a step away from her hiding place, her legs feeling unsteady as she walked toward Logan. She proceeded with caution around the tombstones. Her heart pounded hard against her chest; she was nervous about what was to happen. *Is he going to send me away, or will he embrace me when he sees me?*

Her pace was slow and quiet. She kept walking forward and when she was about thirty feet away from him, she got a glimpse of a man coming out of a vehicle. It momentarily distracted her from her path. She stopped abruptly, turning toward him. For a few seconds he eyed her suspiciously; suddenly a broad smile appeared on his face. He stood erect with his hands by his sides at the limo, not moving. He nodded and she did the same. It was Henry!

She continued as quietly as a mouse until she was ten feet from Logan. The peacefulness of the cemetery was eerie. She could hear the rustle of the leaves in the trees and feel the warm sun on her back. Fright invaded her soul. She was petrified of being rejected by him. She shuddered at the thought. Bailey took another small step forward, then stood there like she had been turned to stone. Her arms were frozen in place at her sides, and her eyes were locked on Logan. She'd finally found him! She had so much love in her heart for him! She swallowed hard, closed her eyes, and said in a frail voice, "Logan."

***

A shiver ran down Logan's body; he twitched for no apparent reason. He then felt a presence behind him, and heard a muffled voice call his name. He swiveled around in his chair to glance behind him. What he saw shocked him; he was overjoyed! He jumped to his feet in disbelief, facing the woman he loved. His mouth opened, but no words came out. *She is here! She came!* He reached up and took off his sunglasses so he could see her in the sunlight. Neither one moved, they just looked at each other. Finally he walked forward until he was a foot away from her. He closed his eyes for just a second as he inhaled her aroma, further evidence she was real. He opened his eyes.

"Bailey..." he murmured. He turned his face away from her with shame for all the pain he had caused her. He felt her velvety hand on his cheek. She gently brought his face to hers. Her touch made him lust for her. He closed his eyes to be able to take it all in. She stroked her fingers down his neck down to his chest. He didn't dare look at her, afraid she might turn and run away. His could smell her lavender scent. She was so close to him. *It can't be! Am I hallucinating?* But when her warm lips touched his and her tongue started to dance to his rhythm, he brought up his arms to embrace her. He could feel her body pressing against his. His desire burned deep inside him, wanting to be free.

He pushed her back to arm's length, with his eyes fixated on her.

"I'm really sorry about everything I put you through. I didn't know anything about those ugly pictures you received. Riker had me drugged, I didn't participate, I..." he tried to explain.

Bailey quieted him by putting her finger on his mouth and said, "Hush! I know that now. That's why I came to find you. The only link I had to you was Riker, and when I heard he'd died, I absolutely had to come. You needed me. I regret rejecting you when you came to me. I love you, and if you'll still have me..."

He grabbed her quickly and held her tight in his arms. He said, "Now that you're here, I'm never letting you go again. I love you, too." His mouth came bearing down on hers once again. Logan was finally happy! His search was over. He had found his true love.

The End

ABOUT THE AUTHOR

Ann El-Nemr started writing a few years ago and this is her fourth book. It started as a hobby, but is now her new career. Her other fiction books are *Betrayed*, *Forgiven* and *The Pledge* which were all published by Jan-Carol Publishing, Inc. There is always component of suspense in her books, accompanied by a dash of romance. Ann loves to surprise her readers with unexpected endings. She enjoys hearing from her fans and can be reached on Facebook, LinkedIn, or at her website, www.annelnemr.com.

BLINDED BY OBSESSION

COMING SOON FROM ANN EL-NEMR

A grief-stricken, young widow named Lucy moves to a new town after the tragic death of her husband. She unexpectedly finds an admirer, Cole, who she eventually falls in love with; but unbeknownst to her, Rodney, a deranged fan, has been stalking her from afar for weeks. Rodney becomes obsessed with Lucy. He's disillusioned and believes she belongs to him and if he can't have her, no one will. Rodney has to decide if he should carry out his twisted plan to kill Cole, Lucy, or both. Will Cole be able to save his love, or will Rodney be captured before he can inflict his wrath on them?

CPSIA information can be obtained
at www.ICGtesting.com
Printed in the USA
FFOW05n1936141015